Dark Chapters:

The Sky will Fall

Darren R Hill

© Darren R Hill 2010
First published 2010
ISBN 978 1 84427 537 3

Scripture Union
207–209 Queensway, Bletchley, Milton Keynes, MK2 2EB
Email: info@scriptureunion.org.uk
Website: www.scriptureunion.org.uk

Scripture Union Australia
Locked Bag 2, Central Coast Business Centre, NSW 2252
Website: www.scriptureunion.org.au

Scripture Union USA
PO Box 987, Valley Forge, PA 19482
Website: www.scriptureunion.org

British Library Cataloguing-in-Publication Data
A catalogue record of this book is available from the British Library.

Printed and bound in the UK by CPI Bookmarque, Croydon, CR0 4TD
Cover design by GoBallistic

Scripture Union is an international charity working with churches in more than 130 countries, providing resources to bring the good news of Jesus Christ to children, young people and families and to encourage them to develop spiritually through the Bible and prayer.

As well as our network of volunteers, staff and associates who run holidays, church-based events and school Christian groups, we produce a wide range of publications and support those who use our resources through training programmes.

For Rebekah, Natasha and Jonathan.
Sorry this took so much time.

Prologue

'Dagon bestows on us divine blessing and favour, but our god also gives us you, Shennahgon.' Seranim Abad leaned toward the soldier standing in front of him. Abad's iron goblet waved erratically in front of him; the wine inside teetering on the brink of escaping, before it sloshed back from the goblet's lip.

Abad's face had a warm glow that had more to do with the wine than the sun's warmth. His eyes fixed on the soldier, whose gaze averted direct contact with the city lord.

'There is no need for false modesty here Shennahgon – Captain Shennahgon, leader of the guard, leader of my army.' Abad paused and took a sip that half-drained his goblet of its contents. A smile stretched the skin across his face, and as he raised his head, the folds under his chin disappeared. Abad, the larger than life ruler of Gaza, and still decadent playboy and spoilt son of Abaddon, had abused his body from excessive wine and food, but he was still young. In fact, a similar age to Shennahgon who stood in front of him.

'If it wasn't for your work, your dedication to Dagon and the devotion to your Seranim, we'd still be at the whim of that animal. Raise your eyes.'

Shennahgon wasn't used to looking directly at the city lord. In fact, as was the same for everyone else, to gaze upon Abad was an insult. And insults were punished. But then, so was disobedience. He raised his head and met the eyes of Abad. The Seranim had a smile on his face and his eyes mirrored the happiness. The wine was obviously having an effect but Shennahgon was a good judge of character and could tell that Abad was offering friendship.

'We all owe you a debt, Captain. Come share your triumph next to me. Sit down and enjoy the celebrations. Our city is safe now; you don't need to be the Captain today.' Abad beckoned to the servants around him to bring some more cushions for Shennahgon to recline on and to bring the Captain his own goblet of wine.

'Today we celebrate, and tomorrow we'll see what reward we can find for the man who captured the beast.' This time as Abad raised his goblet some of the wine escaped and rained onto the cushions surrounding the large leader. 'And Shennahgon, I can heartily recommend the wine.' The laughter was a wheezed effort that sounded more like Abad was choking, but his attendants were unconcerned – they well knew the sound of their leader enjoying himself.

'I apologise that it has taken so long to honour you and arrange this sacrifice to Dagon, but we have been rather busy.' Abad turned and smiled to the other city lords and dignitaries who were seated around him, knowing smiles passing between them. 'But I understand that the animal has been put to good use.'

Shennahgon seated himself on the hastily-brought-forward cushions. It had been several months since the capture and although they had found something to pass the time, Shennahgon thought that Abad and the other Seranims had shown great disrespect to Dagon. He remembered the words of his father, 'If you honour and remember your god, your god will honour and remember you.' He couldn't help feeling that they had neglected to do this.

The wind danced through the columns that stood at the temple's entrance. It skipped past the guards who were on duty, ruffling the feathers that adorned their helmets. As the wind entered the temple, it tugged on the robes and cloaks of the temple priests moving in time with their rituals and rites. It passed by the temple prostitutes, lifting and billowing their fine dresses as they danced with movements, enhanced by the free-flowing wine of celebration. The wind continued across the floor of the temple and Shennahgon watched it lift cloth and dust on its journey until it approached the blinded man, who was now standing between the central pillars, the pillars that supported the roof. The wind swirled around the man, lifting his tattered rags and making them flutter in the breeze. The hair on the man's chest also waved along with the wind.

But as Shennahgon lifted his eyes he watched as the wind had no effect on the man's head. The hair on the man's head remained still. It was damp with perspiration. It clung to the sides of his face. The hair... there was hair on his head.

Shennahgon lifted himself from his seat, spilling the wine that he had been holding. The liquid fell onto Abad whose mouth dropped open in shock at this insult, but before he could call on the guards to punish this uncultured soldier, Abad heard a cry from Shennahgon that chilled him to the bone.

'The hair... why did you let the hair grow back?'

The man between the pillars raised his head. The hair was matted to his head and face, but it was parted enough to reveal his features. The teeth were gritted and the lips slightly parted, in a mouth that grimaced as the body called for strength. But it was the eyes that drew attention.

The face was staring at Abad and the other leaders. Staring, but not looking – or was it? The eyelids were raised, open, revealing the eyes that were within. But there were no ordinary eyes. For a start, these eyes could not see. The eyeballs were disfigured, congealed lumps of flesh. They were scarred white, but veins of blood ran through them, without irises or pupils to focus.

The man's arms were outstretched and were placed firmly on the pillars at the centre of the temple. These pillars supported the whole roof of the temple. And it was an ornate roof. It was painted to resemble the sky. Despite being inside, the roof was painted to look like you were out in the open. Shennahgon looked at the 'roof sky' and began to see the cracks appear, each one snaking a path between the painted clouds. Brick by brick and stone by stone, the sky began to fall.

Shennahgon saw the body. It was between two clouds. As birds often flew between the clouds in the air, the body was flapping in the air too. But that was where the similarity ended. The graceful flight of a bird was in no way matched by the wildly, wheeling arms of the person.

As a child, Shennahgon had often day-dreamed about soaring through the air like an eagle. He would be free of the confines of only being able to walk and run. He would fly from Gaza to Gath and then back out across the sea, gliding down to skim across the water before rising high and seeing the world of Dagon. But the childhood dream was being replaced by the adult living nightmare.

Birds could either glide or flap their wings to move through the air; the body was doing neither. It dropped like the stones around it, along with the clouds that were only light and fluffy in appearance. As the body thudded into the temple floor below, countless bones snapped, severing arteries and rupturing flesh. The scream that had accompanied the descent ended abruptly. Within a moment the body vanished under the clouds, which disintegrated into chunks of rubble as they pulverised the flesh.

More flightless bodies were falling from the sky. Too many people had wanted to be in the temple this day and so they had climbed to the roof and used whatever vantage points they could find. Now they were falling like overripe fruit from a tree, splitting and smashing like fruit hitting the sun-baked paths in the orchards.

Shennahgon's vantage point had provided him with a view of devastation. Now, as the sky roof crumbled, the walls joined the collapse. The whole temple was falling in on itself. His vantage point shook as the wall on which the raised platform was attached began its inward plunge.

Shennahgon heard a scream from behind him. It came from Abad who was unsuccessfully trying to climb from his reclined position. His attendants were attempting to flee, but as the wall lurched, the platform tilted forward and they found themselves losing the battle. Abad finally made it out of his couch as the angle of the platform became so steep that he was rolled onto the floor. Abad looked up at Shennahgon, who was somehow managing to stay upright. He thought the

Seranim looked like a fish floundering out of water; his mouth was opening and closing as if gasping for air.

Shennahgon felt the platform shift once again beneath him. This time he lost balance and fell beside the city lord, Abad. The Seranim looked at Shennahgon pleadingly, and the Captain of the Guard once again averted his eyes. As he did, the platform gave way and they fell to the floor. Not enough to pulverise their bodies as they were far lower than the roof, but enough to take the breath from their lungs. Shennahgon was sure he heard something snap as Abad landed beside him. A sound of pain resonated from Abad to Shennahgon's ears, but the soldier couldn't respond.

He lifted his head and looked toward the man pushing over the columns. The man was sightless and yet Shennahgon was sure that the man was looking directly at him and the fallen city lord beside him.

The columns finally passed the point of no return and came crashing to the ground. And as the column landed on top of Shennahgon, crushing his armour like egg shell, the only thought that went through his mind was that you shouldn't look directly at a Seranim.

PART ONE

The Visitor

The cowled figure sat cross-legged, not motionless, but with minimum movement. It was as though the figure morphed into different positions – melted from hands placed in his lap, to hands clasped in front of his chest. Of course, you couldn't tell the figure was a he, but there weren't many women who sat in front of a fire in the desert.

The fire burned, its flames waving in and out of existence. The day was warm; there was no need for a fire. And the figure wasn't eating. No animal had been held above the flame to cook. In fact the figure hadn't done anything apart from the posture adjustments since it had been noticed.

Zeponeth, the wife of Manoah stood watching the figure. She had been collecting some wheat from the field and had noticed the figure beyond their land. Their land? Well technically yes, but for years now they had been paying tribute to the Philistines. It wasn't a bad situation – the Hebrews paid tribute and the Philistines led and protected them. What was bad though, thought Zeponeth, was the horrendous worship of that Philistine god, Dagon. She knew so many Israelites had abandoned Adonai and turned to worship the disgusting idol. She shuddered as she wondered if the rumours were true, that people sacrificed their children to that false god.

The thought of so many children's lives pointlessly lost made her think of her own family, or lack of it. She had not been able to give her husband a son, or any child. God had not blessed her. The family was wealthy in other areas: the farmland produced well and they had many servants. But there were no children to pass the wealth on to. And Zeponeth wasn't getting any younger.

She lifted her gaze back to where the figure had been sitting, but he was gone, as was the fire. She blinked in disbelief. As she swept her gaze over where she thought the fire was, her eyes saw the figure again. He was walking towards her. Again his movements were fluid. It was as though he was moving with the least amount of effort but getting the most amount of movement possible. The figure almost glided. His long overgarment swept along the sand as he approached, although Zeponeth still couldn't make out the face. The figure had a hood over its head that hid the face from view. However, a hooded face should be in shadow, but she saw no darkness from within the cowl.

The figure was almost to the edge of their farm now, and he was definitely heading straight for Zeponeth. She felt no fear though. In fact she felt a calmness that she hadn't felt for ages. The sadness that had been her companion for years now seemed to have left her as this stranger approached. He was now within their fields and was only a few metres away. The figure stopped.

Zeponeth held her basket of wheat at her side. She looked at the stranger. There was still no fear. In fact she knew, somehow, that this stranger was a man of God, the God who had brought her ancestors from Egypt, the God of Abraham, Isaac and Jacob – their God.

'Welcome to our home. You are our guest. Can I get you some water or food? Or perhaps you need a place to rest.' The offer of hospitality was something Zeponeth's people held dear; not to offer it would be an insult.

The stranger stood before her. Again, with liquid-like movement, he clasped the front of his cowl and lowered the head covering. Zeponeth was transfixed. The stranger was a man, or at least she thought it was. The hair was dark and long, tied away from the eyes with a single golden cord. But despite having long hair, like many of the holy men, the face was completely clear of hair apart from very slim eyebrows. The chin was completely clean, as if no hair had ever grown there. The stranger was obviously old enough to grow a beard but his face showed no signs of ever having bothered. Obviously old enough? Again this wasn't really clear – as Zeponeth looked at the face she realised it had no lines or wrinkles whatever.

But what caught Zeponeth's breath were the stranger's eyes. They were blue, azure blue. This stranger was not local. The eyes also seemed to look right through her. Zeponeth felt that those eyes could see more than what stood before them; she felt her whole life was laid out before him. She felt insignificant, like a grain of sand in the desert, but she held the stranger's gaze.

'You are sterile and childless.' The stranger's voice was neither deep nor high. It was plain and calm. There was no accusation or condemnation in the words he spoke. For the first time Zeponeth felt that being unable to give her husband a child was not her fault. She looked at the stranger as he spoke and saw his eyes glisten. Moisture welled gently in them and a solitary tear rolled down his face. The words the stranger had spoken had caused such emotional pain to him that he had been brought to tears.

Zeponeth lowered her head; she didn't want to see the pain of the stranger and despite not feeling guilty, she could still feel her own pain at not being a mother. She felt a touch on her chin. The stranger had reached out and was now gently raising her head back to look at him.

'You are going to conceive a son.' Again the eyes of the stranger glistened, but this time they were sparkling. At her look of shock and surprise, the stranger nodded.

For the first time in their conversation his expression changed and a smile broke out on his face. Zeponeth's hand had risen to her face and was now held in front of her mouth. She shook her head in disbelief.

The stranger removed his hand from beneath Zeponeth's chin; she had forgotten it was still there. He held it before her face, one finger slightly raised. Here comes the bad news, thought Zeponeth. 'You must drink no wine or fermented drink or eat any unclean food. No razor may be used on his head.' She looked back into his eyes.

'Your son will be a Nazirite, set apart to God from birth.' Zeponeth remembered the laws concerning the Nazirites, but they were normally only for a specific time. Again her head began to shake; she didn't understand what was being said. She looked at the stranger again, with concern in her eyes.

'Your son will begin the deliverance of Israel from the hands of the Philistines.' It was as though the wind had stopped blowing and the world had stopped spinning. Zeponeth would have said that nothing could surpass the news of her giving birth, but this stranger had done just that. The stranger lowered his hand and nodded his head ever so slightly. That nod confirmed all the fear and apprehension the revelation had laid on her heart. The smile was also gone from the stranger's eyes.

In another fluid movement the stranger lifted his cowl and covered his hair. His face was once again hidden in the strange shadow that wasn't dark. He turned around and began to walk back the way he had come. Zeponeth had so many questions running through her mind that she didn't know where to begin. She had just come out to get some wheat and now, all of this. She wanted to thank God; she wanted to ask God why; she wanted to know how; but above all, she wanted to believe.

She looked toward the stranger again and saw that he was once again sitting in front of a fire a way out in the desert. It was as though the conversation had never happened. Everything was back as it was. While she watched, the stranger turned his head toward her and nodded. It was true. Zeponeth dropped her basket and ran to find her husband.

★ ★ ★

Zeponeth burst through the door with such a force that Manoah dropped the stone beads he had in his hand. 'Now look what you've made me do.' Manoah put his hands to his head and tried to remember how many stones were in his hand. 'I was tallying the accounts; now I've no idea where I am.' He shook his head and contemplated starting all over again. He reached across the table and began to claw the stones together.

Manoah sighed deeply. He loved Zeponeth, but she could so easily be distracted. She needed to be far more practical than she was; she was always dreaming about what might be and what might happen. But those things never did occur... like the son he so wanted. He wanted a blessing from God, so that he could pass on this farm to him when he was older. But it seemed they were never going to be blessed in that way. Despite years of trying, there was no sign of a child, none at all. However, Zeponeth was still convinced that she would provide him with a son, and she spoke with that in mind. But Manoah was beginning to realise that it would be one of his household, a servant, who would inherit the land.

Manoah gazed up at his wife, a rueful smile on his lips, and immediately his jaw dropped and his eyes widened. Zeponeth was shaking and her face was drained. Her arm was outstretched, pointing through the door she had just burst through. Her mouth was opening and closing, but no sound came out. She pulled both arms to her mouth, closed her eyes and took a deep breath.

'In the field... Man of God... spoke... sitting down... no beard... looked like an angel... don't know where he's from... or his name... didn't ask... didn't say... he... he...' Zeponeth finally ran out of breath and Manoah took the opportunity to join the conversation.

'What in God's land of milk and honey are you on about, woman? I understood none of that.' Manoah rose from his seat and walked toward his wife, who was again searching for the right words to say and the breath with which to say them. But she gave up trying to speak and instead began to pull at Manoah's cloak. Manoah momentarily held his ground, but seeing the determination in his wife's eyes, he sighed, dropped his head and let her lead him from the room and the tallying of the accounts – they'd have to wait for a while.

Manoah stood at the edge of the field looking out to where Zeponeth said the man was sitting. There was nothing but sand and rocks and a few shrubs that were managing to cling to life in the dry landscape.

'Please, Manoah, you must believe me. He was here. He spoke to me. He said we were going to have a son. That he was going to be a Nazirite to God. I mustn't eat anything unclean or drink any wine; the child is a gift from God. Please – you have to believe me.'

Manoah turned back to his wife and looked into her eyes. They were full of tears. But even through these tears, Manoah could clearly see her eyes. They bore into him with an intensity he had never seen before. Her eyes matched her words and her body language. Each pleaded with Manoah to be believed. He had never seen her this way before.

'But if it is true, then where…' Manoah had only half-heartedly begun the sentence but let it fade off as he saw Zeponeth's eyes well up again until the tears flowed down her cheeks. She turned away from him and stared towards where the man should have been sitting. A gust of wind lifted some of the sand and carried it away. Gone, just like the man.

Manoah put his arm around Zeponeth's shoulder and pulled her toward him as they both stared at the empty field.

'If it is true, then it is true.' Manoah's practicality often frustrated Zeponeth, but this time she felt content. Manoah hadn't dismissed what she had said, and because she knew what had happened that was good enough for her. They would have a child, and that child would bring honour to God and release God's people.

She relaxed in Manoah's hug. 'Thank you.'

Answered prayer

Manoah turned in his bed and decided that sleep was never going to come. He moved his legs from beneath the cover and quietly stood. Zeponeth slept soundly, her face and breathing content, unlike her husband.

Manoah left their bedroom and going straight through the main living area, he headed for the main entrance to their house. He pulled aside the wooden door and left. The sky above was clear and the stars overhead gazed down on the farmer. He looked up at them and thought of all the people in the world who turned to them for help and guidance.

He needed guidance now, but he wouldn't find any in the movements of the stars, nor from the moon which shone from amongst the stars. He thought of the Egyptians, who would turn to the stars, moon and sun – anything, or so it seemed to Manoah – for help.

Manoah was a Hebrew. His ancestors were former slaves of the Egyptians. But Manoah's God had rescued them from slavery and brought them into this land. No god of the Egyptians had been able to stand against the

God of the Hebrews. And it was to this God that Manoah would turn now.

Manoah and his family, including those who worked on the farm for him, had stuck with Adonai, even when so many of their neighbours had turned to Dagon. He believed in the God of the Hebrews' salvation, not the orgies and gluttony of this Philistine idol.

Manoah shook his head as he walked around his house to the closest field. This was a special place. When his father had given him this piece of land, Manoah had thanked both his father and God. The first thing he did was to create a memorial, a physical sign of thanks to God. Manoah now approached this small pile of stones that had stood through wind, rain and sunshine for all the years since.

He fell to his knees and lowered his face so that it touched the ground in front of him. Manoah cried out, 'God of Abraham, God of Jacob and God of Joseph, Saviour of your people in Egypt, my Lord, Adonai: I thank you for all you have provided for my family and for my people.' The dust on the floor around his mouth puffed up as he spoke. 'I ask for forgiveness for all that we have done to anger you; forgiveness from the actions that have handed us over to the Philistines.' Manoah's voice was ragged and was becoming more of a sob as he pleaded for forgiveness.

'And Adonai, I ask you, no, I beg you, let the man of God you sent to us come again. Teach us what we should do, how we should bring the child, the boy, up. Teach us how we should guide the boy who is to be born.' Tears fell from his eyes onto the dusty ground, but these weren't tears of sadness or pain. They were tears of joy and praise to Manoah's God. Manoah realised as he prayed that he believed. All doubt had been removed from his mind and he totally trusted his God.

Manoah was going to be a father. Manoah and Zeponeth were going to have a baby boy. And God would be honoured through this child's actions. And once again God's people would have their own land.

★ ★ ★

As he tended to the plants, Manoah heard shouts and hurried footsteps. The tall grass at the edge of the field was swaying as if in a storm. First it moved one way and then the other, as whatever was causing it to move passed it by. And whatever was causing it to move was heading in Manoah's direction. He squinted his eyes and strained his ears in an effort to make out exactly what was going on.

There was an audible sigh from Manaoah as Zeponeth emerged from the tall grass screaming his name. However, she was so agitated by something, and was so clearly out of breath, that the sound coming from her sounded like a lion roaring. Manoah dropped the wooden farm implement on the ground, picked up his staff and headed to meet his flustered wife.

Through the shrieks, coughs and stammered syllables, Manoah was able to make out that Zeponeth was trying to tell him that the man who had appeared the other day was back. Manoah didn't wait for Zeponeth to regain her breath; he strode off in the direction of their house. He was determined to see this man.

* * *

At the edge of their farm Manoah stopped and looked to the land beyond. Unlike the previous week when he had seen nothing, this time he saw a hooded figure sitting by a fire. He glanced at Zeponeth who had caught up with him and was now bent over drawing in huge amounts of air to regain her calm. As she raised her head, he began to ask, 'Is that...?'

He pointed to the figure and Zeponeth nodded. Despite having run from his field and wanting to know what was going on, Manoah now felt a moment of trepidation. It wasn't exactly fear; it was something deeper. He felt his stomach tighten, and the confidence that had powered his run dissipated. Somewhere in his mind the thought that this was his God at work scared him more than any Philistine militia.

Finding courage from deep within and being pushed by Zeponeth with an arm in his back, Manoah left the farm and headed to the seated figure, although now, and without Manoah noticing, the figure was standing and looking right at them.

Manoah watched as the figure removed the cowl from his head. Like Zeponeth before, Manoah was taken aback by the lack of facial hair. The eyes too looked remarkable to Manoah. They were like pools of clear water, deep and fathomless.

'Manoah of Dan, I suppose you have one or two things you'd like to ask me?' The voice was clear and precise, but with a warmth and richness that immediately put Manoah at ease. The voice continued to reverberate within Manoah's head after the words trailed off. If this man were a prophet, a man of God, then Manoah understood how his voice would command attention.

'Are you the one who talked to my wife?' The farmer's question was little more than rhetorical considering Zeponeth's enthusiasm.

However the stranger answered, 'I am.' At once any doubts Manoah may have had disappeared like a puddle of water evaporating in the hot sun. They were going to have a son. That son was a gift from God and therefore they would bring the child up as God commanded.

'When your words are fulfilled,' Manoah began by showing his faith, 'how do we bring the child up? What is to be the rule for the boy's life and work?'

'As I said before, your wife must do these things. She must not eat anything from the grapevine, nor drink any wine or other fermented drink. And she mustn't eat anything unclean as Moses proclaimed. She must do everything I have commanded.'

'I...' Manoah looked to Zeponeth, who nodded vigorously, '... we understand.' Zeponeth reached toward the stranger with one arm and with the other pointed toward their home. 'Let us share hospitality with you. Stay with us while we prepare a goat for you.' Manoah started toward the house and, directed by Zeponeth, the stranger followed.

'I will not eat your food, but I will stay for a while.' Manoah noticed the way the stranger was walking. His movements seemed fluid and he appeared to move without expending any energy. It was both unsettling and apparently unnatural, and yet completely perfect. Manoah shook his head as his thoughts became jumbled. The stranger seemed to glide up next to him.

'The child will be a gift from Adonai, our God. If you want to prepare a goat then don't do it for me, but as a burnt offering to the Lord.'

Zeponeth prodded Manoah in the ribs and nodded at the stranger. Manoah waved his hand to keep Zeponeth quiet.

'We were wondering, erm, well, when what you say would happen.' Manoah was stammering and struggling for the right words to say, but with another dig in the ribs from his frustrated wife he found them. 'We want to know your name. We want to honour you when the child is born.'

The stranger stopped walking and looked at the soon-to-be parents. They shuffled to a stop, waiting for him to say something.

'Why do you ask my name? It would be too difficult to understand – beyond your tongue.' There was a definite smile as the stranger resumed his progress to the house. Manoah and Zeponeth looked at each other with blank faces for a moment and then followed the stranger.

★ ★ ★

The rock to the side of their house had been used several times over the years to make offerings to their God. The first fruits of the harvest were religiously brought here, and there were several blood stains from previous live sacrifices. The stranger stood to one side, his arms clasped together and his head slightly bowed. He was muttering words that Manoah and Zeponeth didn't recognise.

The goat that Manoah had selected was grazing on some scrub grass, unaware of its role in the ritual about to be performed. Several times, Zeponeth had to coax it away from the grain that was also being offered. Meanwhile, Manoah gathered the tinder sticks and wood to burn the offering. He laid them on the rock and picked up some of the dry scrub that the goat had been nibbling. He stuffed this amongst the wood until he was satisfied that it would act as kindling.

Manoah went into the house and emerged a moment later holding a pot in one hand and a small lamp in the other. He passed the lamp to his wife and approached the altar with the pot. He lifted the dark piece of pottery and carefully poured its contents over the wood and kindling. The pyre glistened with the oil that now clung to the wood.

Manoah lifted his eyes to gaze at the stranger. His head was still bowed and the words were still spilling from his mouth, although Manoah still couldn't make any sense of what was being said. The words sounded like no language he had ever heard, and he had heard plenty. The land that God had given the Hebrews was central to many trade routes, and the traders of many nations had passed through it. The stranger's words weren't like any of the languages the traders had used. Manoah wondered if it was any language at all; the words flowed more like music than a conversation.

He picked up the small sheaf of wheat and laid it across the top of the shining pyre. As he placed the wheat down, he thanked the God of Abraham, Jacob and Isaac for all the blessings that had been giving to them: the farm and the harvest of wheat of which this was a small token of thanks.

Manoah went to where the goat was grazing and brought it before the altar. He stepped over the animal with one leg and, from inside his cloak, Manoah removed a short-bladed knife. The light from the evening sun caught the sharp edge of the stone blade.

With one quick movement Manoah lifted the head of the goat with his left hand. His right hand brought the knife to the animal's throat and swiftly pulled it across, severing the arteries and windpipe. The goat twitched once and then again as the blood pumped from the cut in its neck. Then it stirred no more, its life extinguished. The sacrifice wasn't just the life of an animal. For Manoah and his household, the offering of a precious animal wasn't an easy gift. All the livestock that Manoah had was extremely valuable. But Manoah's God was worthy of such an offering.

He lifted the animal onto the stone altar, it's limp body manipulated into position on top of the wheat and wood. The animal, though stained with the blood that had kept it alive, gave the impression of completeness and peace to the ceremony.

Zeponeth handed the lamp back to Manoah, its flame now throwing light onto the proceedings as the sun set deeper. Evening had arrived while the offering was taking place and now the darkness of the night was taking hold. But there was no cold in the air. The day had been warm and the evening was holding onto that warmth.

Manoah stepped forward. 'Adonai, we thank you for your promise to Abraham that his descendents would number more than the stars in the sky. And we thank you that you have said, through your servant, that we will continue that blessing with a son of our own.' Tears of joy began to run down Zeponeth's face as her husband lent forward and touched the flame of the lamp to the offering pyre.

At once the dry timber caught and the flame spread beneath the wheat and goat. The evening scene was lit and Manoah and Zeponeth lowered their heads and muttered further prayers of thanks to their God. Meanwhile, the flames rose and began to burn the offerings placed on the stone altar and, as they did so, the smoke lifted into the night sky, rising toward the stars that shone.

Manoah felt a tap on his arm and lifted his head to see what Zeponeth wanted. She pointed ahead of her. The stranger had disappeared. He had been there moments before. Manoah could remember seeing him as he was preparing the offering, but now, where he had been standing, there was nothing.

Manoah turned back to his wife to ask where the stranger had gone. But his question was choked off as he saw his wife's face. The flames from the altar were deep orange and were throwing an amber hue all around them, but Zeponeth's face was a ghostly white. She was no longer looking at where the stranger had been but at the offering itself. Her mouth hung open in a look of total shock.

Manoah slowly turned his head. He looked at the altar and the offering burning upon it and then followed the flames as they rose into the air, carrying the smoke upward. But the smoke wasn't the only thing rising from the offering. The stranger appeared to be hovering above the burning animal and grain, and seemed to be flickering like the flame.

Manoah realised that he could see through parts of the stranger, or he thought he could, because as he tried to focus on one part of the body, it became solid and another part became translucent. Manoah couldn't understand what he was seeing. The stranger's body was like the flame and smoke of the offering and, like those, it was rising higher into the air. As it rose, it became less and less solid, until it finally disappeared completely.

Manoah and Zeponeth fell face down to the ground. For once neither of them looked at each other before acting. They buried their heads into the sandy earth, hiding their faces from the vision that had taken place before them. Their whole bodies shook with fear at what they had just witnessed. Muffled pleas for salvation and protection from God rose into the air as they expected their lives to be extinguished at any moment.

When nothing happened for a few minutes, Manoah slowly raised his head. The burnt offering continued to burn, but the stranger was nowhere to be seen and nothing else untoward was happening either. He lifted his body until he was sitting on his knees looking at the altar. 'He gave us a message from God.' Manoah was talking to both Zeponeth and himself, reasoning out what had happened. 'God's messenger.' The logic of the situation played out in Manoah's spoken thoughts. 'That was an angel of the Lord.'

As this realisation sank in, the implications rose in Manoah's mind. No one could see God and survive. Their God was unseen, unlike the idols that others worshipped. But they had seen God's own messenger, God's angel. The implication was clear in Manoah's head: they would now surely die. It was a simple matter of time before the flames that had risen in offering were returned to consume Manoah and his wife. 'We have seen God, so we will die.'

Zeponeth was not normally level-headed when it came to working things out. She was impulsive and her conclusions often left Manoah dumbfounded. 'But God accepted the offering.' Her words stopped Manoah in his macabre acceptance of the situation. 'God accepted the goat and the grain. If Adonai wanted to kill us he would not have accepted the offering.'

Manoah realised that, for once, his mind had raced and come to a pretty unrealistic conclusion. But the events of the day and evening had left him more than a little distrustful of reality. He had come face to face with the angel of the Lord, and had so far survived. Zeponeth's words also made sense – the offering had been accepted like Abel's and unlike Cain's, the sons of Adam.

Zeponeth held Manoah's shaking hands and looked him in the eye. The air was still warm and the burning offering added to the heat in the air, but they both shivered with fear and trepidation.

'And more importantly, husband,' she held his hand tighter and a smile emerged on her face, 'we're going to have a son.'

Manoah nodded and he too began to grin. 'I'm going to be a father.' They fell into each other's arms and held on for dear life. Tears flowed from both pairs of eyes, but they were tears of joy.

'You'd best start building a cot.'

Manoah laughed; there was his wife rushing her thoughts into the future again.

Boys will be boys

The baby was wrapped in cloth and handed to an exhausted, but elated, Zeponeth. She looked at the child in her arms and smiled. Its hair was so fine that it looked as though it had none. The baby's eyes were shut tightly and it was unable to see anything of this new world it had been born into.

The newborn struggled in her arms, trying to wriggle free of the cloth it was wrapped in, but Zeponeth's arms held it tightly. It couldn't free itself. The child's strength was no match for the loving mother, protecting and keeping the baby warm.

The Hebrew midwife smiled at the new mother and child. 'He looks like a born fighter, the way he's struggling there. And the way he was delivered so quickly. You'd think he was on a mission from the Lord himself, the way he came out. I tell you now he won't hang around and wait for others. He's going to be one who gets things done.' The midwife laughed as she continued to tidy up and finish her job.

Zeponeth heard the words and took them deep into her heart. She also remembered what the angel of the

Lord had said, that this child would begin the deliverance of Israel. So far it seemed that the baby was living up to expectations. Like all mothers, Zeponeth thought her baby was special, but unlike all mothers, they hadn't been visited by God's messenger to tell them so.

Zeponeth gazed at the baby in her arms. It no longer struggled and it was looking straight up at her face. She lifted her hand to reach for the baby's face, but for a moment, Zeponeth's breath caught in her throat.

The image of the helpless baby was replaced by a helpless man – a strong muscular man – but like the child in her arms, bald and helpless. The man gazed, but saw nothing; his eyes had been removed. The empty sockets were clotted with drying blood and red, raw flesh. Fear was etched on his face and something else too. Zeponeth couldn't make out what else she was seeing, but as the expression on the face developed, she realised it was regret. The man had done something wrong and that was why he was in this predicament. Despite having no eyes, the man was weeping. Tears flowed from the empty sockets creating red rivulets down his cheeks.

Zeponeth closed her eyes tightly and reopened them. The harrowing vision was gone and once again she gazed on the face of the newborn child.

'Have you got a name yet?' The midwife was still busying herself in the room. Zeponeth had completely forgotten she was still there.

'Yes, his name is Shimshon.'

The midwife nodded and spoke as she continued to clean away, 'Ah yes – a good name. I'm sure he will be radiant and mighty, just like the sun. Perhaps he will be a light to our people.' The midwife stopped her cleaning for a moment and her cheery demeanour disappeared. 'And perhaps he just might be the one to free us from those stinking depraved Philistines!' The midwife emphasised each syllable at the end of her sentence. She let out a huge sigh and then resumed her clearing up.

Zeponeth remembered the words of God's messenger and felt a peace surround and envelope her, but her thoughts were still uneasy as the vision of the helpless man niggled at the back of her mind.

* * *

The old man sat outside the trading hut in the village. His white hair emerged like wisps of smoke from beneath the turban that protected him from the sun's heat. The lines on his face hinted at the unlimited memories deep within.

He sipped the drink that the trader had given him. It was bitter but refreshing. Its bitterness matched the feelings flowing through his body. A small contingent of

Philistine soldiers and a caravan of Philistine families had recently arrived in the village. And now some of them were approaching the trading hut.

'Why have you forgotten your people, O Lord? You are everlasting, but you have forgotten us. You have handed us into the hands of these unbelievers.' His words were muttered, but as the leader of the soldiers passed, he could hear enough to understand. He stopped and looked down at the old man. He signalled to one of the other soldiers who walked back to one of their carriages, climbed inside and emerged a moment or two later with something in his hand.

The soldier handed something to the captain and then stepped back.

'Perhaps you have backed the wrong deity? Next time, find a god who you can rely on, who won't forget you.' The Captain threw something toward the old man and it landed in his lap. Laughing, the Captain moved on into the trading place.

The old man looked into his lap and saw the idol staring back at him. Its crude features, in fact, its very existence, was an abomination to the old Hebrew. He looked to one side and saw a small rock by his feet. He reached over and picked it up. He swung the rock at the idol and it connected with a force which even the old man found surprising. The idol shattered into several pieces and flew into the middle of the sand-covered road.

The pieces of the idol just missed the four boys who were running down the street. Three continued on their run, but one stopped and looked at the pieces. He leant down to take a closer look and then shook his head. He looked to the sky, 'Lord save us!' The old man watched and felt a warmth fill his being. Perhaps all was not lost; if the young still believed, there was still hope.

The boy looked over to the old man and shouted, 'Yahweh has not forgotten us.' The boy ran off after his friends, who were now further down the road playing their game. The old man watched the boy run along. The boy was quite muscular for his age, about 10 years old. But that wasn't the most striking thing about his appearance. It was the long braids of hair that hung down from his head. It had been a long time since he'd seen someone who had taken the Nazirite vow, and he could never remember seeing a Nazirite so young.

'Forgive me, Adonai. Your servant is old and wisdom seems to have escaped me in my age.' The old man finished his prayer with a smile to the heavens – the smile an admission of his own stupidity and lack of faith. As if God could forget his people.

* * *

A gust of wind rushed through the village and Shimshon felt energised by its power. He was with his friends and they were enjoying their game. The wind whipped against their clothes and blew their hair in all directions, apart from Shimshon. His hair was long and braided. The heavy braids would need more than a gust of wind to move them.

They were playing, as they always seemed to, Yeshua's conquest of the Promised Land. It was strange, but whenever they played together, Shimshon always seemed to be Yeshua and the victorious Hebrews. It was his friends, those who were smaller than him, who played the parts of the Amorites, Perizites and all the 'ites' that God removed from the land.

This time it was the battle of Jericho, an old favourite, but one of the most amazing victories God had handed to the Hebrews. Shimshon's friends were stuck in the 'city' as Shimshon marched around them, his hands pretending to hold a musical horn that, on the seventh time around, would signal the fall of the city... and the fun! Well, they were boys.

Shimshon had immersed himself in the game, so it was his friends who noticed the small group watching them. As Shimshon circled his playmates, watching their faces, he suddenly realised that their expressions of fear were genuine and not to do with the game.

'Hey, Hebrew, why aren't you helping your father tend his land to pay the tribute to our king.'

Shimshon stopped his march around the pretend city and slowly turned in the direction his friends were looking. There in front of them, were a group of Philistine teenagers and children. They had arrived with the others and were looking for something to do while the soldiers and their families did their business. And they had found Shimshon and his friends.

There were six of them – all, apart from one, a few years older than Shimshon and his friends. Even though Shimshon was bigger than his friends, these Philistines were bigger still. The Hebrews weren't at war with the Philistines; the uneasy truce was obtained by the Hebrews bowing to Philistine rule, and bowing meant paying them tribute – money.

Shimshon stood in front of his friends, between them and the Philistine group. His hands were still pretending to hold the horn, so he lowered them to his side. They continued to tingle with power and his eyes returned the glare of the older boys.

He readied the saliva in his mouth and spat it out onto the ground in front of him. 'There is my tribute to your Seranim. Do you think that is enough or would he like some more? I have plenty.' He opened his mouth to reveal more spit.

It was shock that stopped any reprisal from the Philistine youths. They didn't want a fight, merely some fun, but this kid seemed like he wanted to take them all on.

It was shock that left Shimshon standing on his own. When he had spat and retorted, the friends he had been playing with disappeared faster than a goat being chased by a lion. All Shimshon heard was the scuffle of feet behind him and the cries of his friends as they ran away. He didn't need to look behind him to confirm that he was now alone. All of a sudden Shimshon's bravado was evaporating.

'Oh, your friends seem to have deserted you. Would you like to review your offer of a tribute in the light of your revised circumstances?' The group laughed at the lonely Hebrew in front of them, and patted themselves on the back for being Philistines.

Shimshon was still tingling and he felt the power coursing through him. He had prayed each day for God to give him the strength to stand up to these unbelievers. He also knew that one day he would help God rid these people from the Promised Land; his parents had been open and honest about why he had had such a strict religious childhood. But something didn't feel right now. It wasn't that his friends had gone – they wouldn't have been much good in a fight anyway – it was more to do with the time not being right. He couldn't understand things exactly, but he was sure that this was the only sign of rebellion he would show today. But what to do about the Philistines in front of him?

'Well little one, although you do seem unnaturally large for a young boy and a Hebrew boy at that; Hebrews are normally so stunted,' one of them taunted. Shimshon felt the words cut deep and he gripped his hands into fists. 'Is there anything you'd like to say or do? How about a proper tribute for your masters?'

Shimshon's anger burst out, 'You are all dogs! I won't even give you the spit left in my mouth.'

This time neither party was hindered by the shock of the outbursts and both groups took steps toward each other – someone was going to get hurt.

The small silver coin landed in front of the group of youths and stopped them immediately. Shimshon saw the coin too and halted his advance. 'There's the tribute for your king – now go and help your parents unload their goods.' Both the Philistines and Shimshon turned to see an old priest walking toward them, his long staff both keeping him upright and aiding his momentum. His priestly robes flowed to the ground and lifted a cloud of dust as he walked.

The hand of the priest rested itself on Shimshon's shoulder. At that exact moment, the tingling within stopped and Shimshon's anger dissipated. 'Come and walk with me young man; these Philistines were returning to their parents, weren't you?' The youths stood their ground for a moment and then picked up the coin and walked away.

The youngest of the group trailed and took a last look over his shoulder at the Hebrew being led away by the priest. He was years younger than the other boys, but they let him tag along because of who he was. His father was the Captain of the Guard, the top man in the Philistine army. His name was Shennahgon; one day he hoped to follow in his father's footsteps. He stared at the strange boy – he would teach Israelites like this some respect when he was older.

Despite the old priest's apparent frailty, Shimshon could feel an inner strength in the way the fingers gripped his shoulder and guided him in the opposite direction. 'Sometimes it is best to walk away and fight another day.' Shimshon looked up at the old man, who was using his staff on one side for support, and the young boy on the other. 'You need to know when to stand and fight and when to wait and hold back.'

'But the Philistines shouldn't be ruling us and taking money from us. And you gave them that coin.' The phrases shot out from Shimshon like a volley of arrows from an advancing army.

The priest slowed his walk and looked at Shimshon with a wry smile on his face. 'Well, the coin that I threw to the Philistines was one of their own.' Shimshon screwed his face up to show he had no idea what the old man was talking about. 'I found the coin as I entered the village. It was on the floor and must have been dropped by their parents when they arrived. So I was only giving them what was rightfully theirs.'

Shimshon smiled as well but he wasn't quite finished yet, 'God gave us this land when he saved us from the rule of the Egyptians. We should be taking it back from them; that is God's will.'

At this, the priest did stop. 'If you are claiming to know God's will, you need to be very careful young man. If you get that wrong you are guilty of using the name of God falsely. That's one of the commandments Moses gave us.'

The old priest began his walk again. 'On this though, I think you may be right. It is God's will that we have this land, but a responsibility comes with that and we haven't played our part. As a nation we have done evil in God's sight and for that God has given control of the land to the Philistines. It has been taken from us.'

Shimshon saw the sadness on the old man's face as the words were spoken. 'So we should take it back!' The zeal in Shimshon returned and for a moment he thought the priest would agree.

The old man looked thoughtful and began to nod. 'Yes, we should take it back.' The old priest's grip tightened on Shimshon's shoulder just in case the young boy was about to take on the group of youths. 'But at the right time. And that is for God to decide.'

They had reached the well in the village and the priest sat down beside it. He motioned for Shimshon to sit before him and the young boy obeyed; Shimshon was used to listening to the priests teach. 'When our people were in Egypt and they were being oppressed by Pharaoh and his people, they lifted their voices to Adonai for help. But it took many, many years for Moses to be called and to lead God's people to freedom.' The priest was using his staff to mark some shapes on the sand while continuing his words. 'The point is, my young friend, that God chooses the right time to act. I can see you are strong and one day may well be a mighty warrior for God, but at the moment those youths would have hurt you... or worse.'

Shimshon grudgingly agreed but wouldn't say that out loud to the priest.

'When the time comes, you'll know. You'll know when to act and what to do.' The priest got up and began to walk away from where Shimshon had sat. 'Trust in God, my friend, and then at the right time you'll know what to do.'

Shimshon stood and was about to follow the priest when he noticed the markings on the ground that had been made by the staff. The priest had drawn a valley and some simple stick people stuck at the bottom of it. Shimshon had no idea what the image meant, but something was telling him that one day he would.

The priest was gone. Shimshon hadn't seen him go, but now that he looked he couldn't find him. Perhaps the old man was not as slow at walking as he had appeared. Shimshon laughed out loud and began to run for home: 'Adonai Tzur Israel.' His God was the rock of his people.

PART TWO

And so it begins

The journey was long and tiring, at least for Shimshon it was. For other traders who crossed the country day after day and month after month, it was a short and simple trip. The donkey that drew his cart was old and its only concern with the commerce that it pulled, was that if it did this job it would be fed. For Shimshon, he had less interest in commerce than the donkey. The donkey had been bred for this and had no other option than to haul the goods from one place to another.

But Shimshon was not bred for this, and that simple fact made him the most miserable of people on the roads, and the trader who very few other traders would want to pass the time of day with. The journey was not only long and tiring but also mind-numbingly boring. And each time Shimshon walked this route, he cried out to his God in prayer, the same prayer over and over, 'How long must I do this, Lord?'

From an early age, Shimshon had been told of the miraculous circumstances of his birth. He had been told that he would begin the setting free of his people from the yoke of the Philistines. He had had to endure the strict religious upbringing imposed by his parents to keep him 'pure' for the work ahead. But where was this work? Surely he wasn't going to set Israel free by hauling this cart every few weeks or tending his father's crops in the intervening weeks.

But Shimshon kept on believing. He would pray each and every day. He would follow the commandments God had given to Moses. And above all else, he would trust in God. But he was also a young man and like everyone else, he was in no way perfect.

Since the time he spoke with the priest many seasons ago, nothing had happened in his life of any interest. He had very few friends and those he had thought his parents were religious nuts. As for a wife, all the eligible Jewish girls were kept a long distance from him by their parents.

Shimshon arrived in Timnah, a small trading village, but with a lot of business. The worst thing for Shimshon was that it had a large population of Philistines. The donkey gave him a dejected look.

'Yeah, I feel the same way too – can't say I like this place either.' Shimshon led the donkey and cart toward the centre of the village. Here he would be able to sell the grain that had come from his parents' farm. If the place wasn't too busy, he might be able to be on his way before the sixth hour.

The village trading centre was full of traders and buyers, each vying for the best deal of the day. As the tall, muscular figure of Shimshon approached, they made way for him and within a few moments he had the buyers' attention.

★ ★ ★

And so the end of another pointless journey, thought Shimshon. At least when he got back, his parents would be pleased as he'd managed to get a better than usual price on the grain that he'd hauled across country.

He wondered if the buyer had been intimidated by his size. Shimshon wasn't a giant like some of the men from Gath, but he wasn't average either. He was big and muscular and, with the uncut hair on his head, he presented quite an imposing figure.

'Time to head home, my good friend.' The donkey responded by snorting from one end and having a bowel movement from the other. 'Yeah, pretty much how I feel about today.' Shimshon shook his head and turned away from the beast.

His eyes swept across the road and he saw her. Shimshon never had time for girls, even if they had been interested in him. His work on the farm and his desire to fulfil his destiny kept him away from pretty much any sort of social life.

But she captivated him. She was with, he assumed, her father and they were trading like everyone else. There were several others in their group who were doing the heavy work of moving the goods around. The girl and her father stood to one side. He was ordering the others to move the contents of their carts to one side. She stood by his side, silently.

She was clothed in a long flowing gown of a high quality. She was also covered pretty much from head to toe. But what captivated Shimshon were her eyes. They were stunning, and despite her clothing being brightly coloured, it was her eyes that stood out. They were green like emeralds and sparkled in the daylight. And they were looking at him.

Shimshon realised that he was staring and that his mouth was open and dribbling slightly. He must have looked as much of an animal as the donkey beside him. He quickly closed his mouth and wiped it with the back of his hand.

He saw the girl raise her hand to her covered face and noticed that her shoulders were shaking. Shimshon realised that she was laughing, and laughing at him. The laughing increased when she noticed that Shimshon had gone bright red.

The girl's father saw what she was doing and what, or rather who, had caught her attention. He said something to her and motioned with his hands for her to move. She bowed her head and began to walk off behind the cart with its goods. As she did, she looked at Shimshon one more time and sneaked a little wave at him, away from the view of her father.

Shimshon wasn't quite sure what had happened, but he felt something that he had never felt before. His history with girls was non-existent, but he seemed to have made an impression on this one.

One of the buyers was walking past him and he grabbed the top of the man's arm.

'Aargh, let go you lumbering fool, you're hurting me.' Shimshon didn't know how strong he had become over the last few years. The buyer rubbed his arm and grimaced in pain as Shimshon released his grip.

'You don't know your own strength, do you, Hebrew?'

Shimshon apologised; something he rarely did. What was happening to him? 'I'm sorry. I just wanted to ask a question.'

'Well you didn't have to break my arm in the process.'

'I am truly sorry. I just wanted to know who that trader is over there – the wine merchant.' The buyer followed Shimshon's gesture and nodded. He then saw the girl who was peeking out from behind the cart.

'Why, you are a sly one, aren't you?' The buyer didn't wait for a reply as he chuckled and gave Shimshon a knowing look. The buyer was from the East, not local and not a Philistine. If he had been, then Shimshon may well have taken issue with him.

'That's Makros, the Vintner, or the Tishbite as his kind call him. And that's his eldest daughter. She'll make a fine bride for someone one day, but not you, my Hebrew friend.' Shimshon questioned the buyer's comment by screwing up his face in a what-are-you-on-about gesture.

'She's a Philistine, my young Hebrew. The chances of you two getting together would be an act of the gods.'

Shimshon physically sighed as his hopes and dreams were instantly deflated. He should have known that such good fortune wouldn't come his way. But the trader had continued talking and Shimshon had not heard his words.

'Sorry, what did you just say?'

'I said, that it would be an act of the gods for you two to get together, or in your case, my Hebrew friend, an act of God! I bid you peace and fulfilment as you journey through life, but I fear she is one piece of fulfilment you will never have.' The buyer went on his way chuckling to himself and shaking his head at the predicament of the Hebrew who had fallen for the Philistine.

Shimshon couldn't understand what he was feeling. He was torn between being physically attracted to the girl and repelled by the fact she was a Philistine, although he knew that the animosity between the two nations was more from his side. The Hebrews should be ruled by Adonai; they were not to submit to any other lord. More and more recently, there had been a lot of mixing with each other, in trade and in marriage, although these things were highly frowned upon by the more devout religious people among them.

But underneath all this, it was the words of the buyer that had made the biggest impression on him, and was also stirring an idea within. 'An act of God' had been his words. Shimshon wondered if God was beginning to act. Was this the time when Shimshon would begin to torment the Philistines?

Shimshon led the donkey and cart from the village to begin the journey back to his home town and the farm. As he trudged down the road, he looked back. The village looked quiet like a ghost town and there was no one in sight. All the trading was going on in the centre, unlike the bigger cities where a lot of business took place at the city gates.

Above the village the clear sky was darkening. Clouds were billowing up and the weather was turning. Shimshon thought how odd this was. The weather never changed in this way. Yes, it may become cloudy or the sun may break through a darkened sky, but that took time. This was happening before his eyes. The clouds were changing from white, to grey, to near black. There was going to be a storm.

It wasn't just the village. The clouds were gathering above Shimshon too. The donkey felt the change as well. It pulled at the reins Shimshon was using to guide it, although the donkey's strength was no match for Shimshon.

'It's only a storm, it'll pass.' Shimshon's consoling did little to allay the donkey's fears, and Shimshon himself was less than convinced at his words. The darkness was now all around them and spreading. Within minutes it stretched as far as he could see and then...

'Craaaack!' The lightning bolt lit the surrounding area and the noise made Shimshon raise both his hands for protection, and he clasped his ears as the sound rung around the area. As he lost the reins, the donkey bolted and set off toward home, with the cart the only thing holding him back.

The old tree that stood just outside the village was ablaze. The lightning had been attracted to it and had released its full force on the old rotting wood. From the village the locals and the visiting traders came running to see what had happened.

Shimshon was some distance off now, but he could hear their words.

'It's a sign!'

'Dagon is not pleased.'

'Quick, someone make an offering to the gods!' Shimshon thought about their words. He knew that it wasn't anything to do with Dagon, but it may be a sign. He turned round quickly and almost knocked the old man onto the ground.

'Now that's no way to rush into things. What did I tell you about knowing when and where to act?' Shimshon couldn't believe it. It was the old priest who he had met all those years before. He had looked ancient the last time they had met, but now the wrinkles were deeper and his weathered skin thinner.

'Yes, it could be a sign. Perhaps the time is right for something to happen, or someone to make it happen.' The old priest looked Shimshon up and down. He then raised his walking staff and jabbed it into Shimshon's stomach.

'Hey, what do you think you're doing?'

'It didn't hurt, did it?' The priest chuckled to himself at some personal joke.

'Well, no, it didn't, but you can't go around hitting people like that.' Shimshon was indignant and a little ashamed that he was being hit by such a frail old man.

'You've grown and become stronger. You've become quite a man. I suppose you'll be wanting a bride now?' The question was rhetorical, but it made Shimshon think of the Philistine girl.

'You should look for signs from God. You never know when the time will be right, but God does. Trust in God. Accept that God knows when things should happen and when they shouldn't.' Once again the old priest looked Shimshon up and down. This time, when he raised his staff, Shimshon used his hand to make sure it didn't connect with him.

'And looking at you I'd say you were quite ready. Perhaps this is the time God has chosen for you to begin your confrontation?' The smile on Shimshon's face grew and grew and he began to nod in agreement.

'If I were you, I'd look for a way to get amongst them and cause some trouble, but be careful. Take it slowly and remember everything you've learned.'

'Thank you, er…' Shimshon didn't know what to say; he felt like a weight had been lifted from his shoulders.

'Don't thank me. It's Adonai you should thank. Now go on, stop wasting time. You've seen the sign and I think you also know what to do.'

Shimshon thanked the old priest once again, then apologised, and then ran off down the road toward home. He had a plan to put into action, although, first of all, he should find where the donkey had got to.

★ ★ ★

'But she is the daughter of the uncircumcised Philistines! Must you find a wife from them?'

The argument had been going on for a while. Shimshon had retuned home after finding the donkey and explained to his parents that he had found the woman that he wanted to marry. She was the daughter of a vineyard owner and seeing as he was the son of a farmer, it would be a good move for both families if he married her. Similar marriages were happening all across the land.

'What about our relatives? Hannah, from your father's family, has a wonderful daughter and she hasn't been betrothed to anyone yet.' Shimshon's mother had never been one for pushing him into things, but all of a sudden she was very keen on him finding a wife among the Hebrews.

'Or why not take a journey to Jerusalem, stay there for a while and look for a wife among your own kind – anything but a Philistine.' Manoah's words were losing authority and he knew it. His son was a headstrong and stubborn man. Once he had set his mind to something, it couldn't be shifted; he took after his mother in that respect.

'She is the right one. I want you to arrange the marriage with her family.'

There was finally silence from his parents. Manoah and Zeponeth looked at each other. His mother was the first to look down and he could see the argument was won. They would get ready and journey to Timnah as soon as possible and arrange the marriage. Manoah nodded and walked away to begin preparations to leave the next day, with a few servants, and start the negotiations.

Shimshon knew they were disappointed but what they didn't know was that this was the beginning of the end for the rule of the Philistines over the Hebrews.

* * *

Shimshon knew the beast was there before there had been the slightest of sound. He hadn't heard, seen or smelt anything, but he knew.

He stopped his clamber over the rocks, raised and turned his head slightly. He breathed in the air, and, with his mouth open, tasted as well as smelled the atmosphere around him. There was just the slightest scent of an animal, a wild animal. From the smell he knew it was a carnivore, the fetid odour unmistakable.

As he stood still he could just make out the noise of something brushing its way through the shrubbery above and behind him. This was a clever beast and a dangerous beast. Shimshon shifted his weight, so that he could turn in an instant, and waited. The shuffling was getting closer and Shimshon noticed that he could hear no other wildlife in the vicinity. The birds had stopped their chatter. The attack was imminent.

'Lord, give me your strength and power.' Shimshon silently raised his request. He was afraid. He was sure God had given him a mission, but an attack by a wild animal here would surely end in death. But how could God allow that? It just didn't make sense. As he prayed, a feeling of calm rose within. He was sure his body was tingling; his muscles, though tense, felt relaxed and ready.

When the attack finally came, it felt like time stretched out. Shimshon heard the roar and then the sound of bushes being blasted aside. Almost instantly Shimshon turned and raised his hands. A lion came flying through the air, its jaw open and teeth bared. Having used its paws to push off from the ledge above, the lion was now bringing them forward, claws extended and glinting in the sunlight. The beast was huge and Shimshon knew that any extended fight would end in a macabre, grizzly manner, with him the defeated.

The lion's jaw widened and Shimshon could see the saliva on each of the fangs. Its head tilted to one side, ready to clamp. This would be quick.

Shimshon attacked. As the lion got to touching distance, instead of trying to fend off the beast, Shimshon thrust his hands into its open mouth. One hand grasped the top jaw of the beast; the other gripped the lower. The momentum of the lion's leap drove Shimshon backward, but he didn't loosen his grip. He could feel the lion's paws hit his body and needles of pain ignited as the claws found purchase.

The Hebrew flexed his muscles, and with all his energy, he pulled his hands in opposite directions. The roar of the lion was still issuing forth as the noise of ligaments ripping and bone splintering began. As Shimshon pulled his hands further apart, the skin around the lion's mouth ripped. Blood now mixed with the beast's saliva as the lion and Shimshon fell backward. Even with his footing gone, Shimshon continued to pull. As the two of them hit the ground, there was an almighty crack – something had broken. Together they rolled down a short incline and came to rest in a heap of blood and dust.

The only pain Shimshon felt was where the lion's claws had bit into his flesh. The pain was still there because the lion's paws were still there. For a moment the Hebrew thought it was all over. The lion had him in its grip and its jaw would soon find his neck, but nothing happened. Shimshon realised he had shut his eyes as the two of them had tumbled. He opened them now and was greeted with a horrifying sight.

Shimshon still held the upper and lower jaws of the lion, but they were no longer connected in any meaningful way. Sinew, ligament and blood were the only evidence that the pieces of jaw belonged to the same animal. The upper jaw, and the rest of the lion's head was still connected to its body, but the angle showed that the animal's neck had been broken. Shimshon had pulled the lion's head apart and snapped its neck like it was a tiny goat.

He let go of the jaw pieces and lifted the paws of the dead beast from his shoulders, careful not to rip his own flesh with the embedded claws. The beast was on top of him and he now pushed it off and rolled himself away from the scene of carnage. What power could have enabled him with such strength? And then he remembered his prayer. He closed his eyes, calmed his breathing and uttered a prayer of thanks.

He heard the sound of running water and found a small brook a hundred or so cubits from the scene of the fight. He knelt down at its side and bathed his wounds and cleaned the remnants of the attack from his flesh. Shimshon breathed deeply and as he exhaled, a broad grin covered his face. He made his hands into fists and flexed his muscles; he felt the power flow through him. He dunked his head into the brook and then lifted it out, flicking his braided hair over his head. The water flew behind him, and as it did, he roared.

At the bottom of the valley, Shimshon's parents heard the sound of a wild animal. 'I hope Shimshon is alright,' Zeponeth said to Manoah. Shimshon's father looked in the direction of the sound, a concerned look on his face.

Shimshon was a good cubit-and-a-half taller than Manoah, but the land around here held many dangers, which was why Shimshon had been scouting ahead.

Manoah was about to call one of the servants to find Shimshon when the bushes to their side rustled and out came a bounding Shimshon, his face a little flushed, but, apart from that, a picture of health.

'Is everything alright?' asked Zeponeth. Shimshon came up beside her, put his arm around her and lifted her off the floor. 'Everything is fine, mother, absolutely fine.'

'Put me down, Shimshon. You don't know your own strength.'

Shimshon smiled and thought, oh but I do! I do know my own strength.

* * *

The young girl was laughing again behind her veil. It seemed that this was a common occurrence for her. Since Shimshon and his family entourage had arrived, everything had gone well. The girl's family had been welcoming and her father was as practical as Manoah.

Despite an initial wariness, it wasn't every day a band of Hebrews arrived at the vineyard of a Philistine and things had progressed well. Both the fathers had immediately seen the potential for their son and daughter to join together in marriage. The merger wasn't just a physical one; Manoah's farm and the Philistine's vineyard would make a powerful business enterprise, ensuring both families would be well supported.

Even Zeponeth had begun to see the positives in the union, although she still harboured deep fears too. As the day progressed, and the conversations between Manoah and the Philistine continued, Zeponeth got to know the women in the family a little better, although she never got to meet the daughter. She was being kept away as was the tradition.

Finally, the negotiations were over and the arrangements had been sealed over a meal. At last Shimshon and the rest of the family got to meet the girl who had inspired these events.

'Ba'alshada is my eldest daughter and she will make your son a fine wife.' Makros, the Timnite, raised a cup of wine and Manoah joined him to seal the deal. Shimshon looked at his future bride and again she giggled behind her veil. Her sister, sitting beside her, was also giggling.

Shimshon was still captivated by her beauty and knew that, while he was tormenting the rest of the Philistine people, he would be happy with her. She would make a good wife and perhaps their family would become great in this land. The marriage would mean that Ba'alshada would become one of them and follow the Hebrew ways and customs and also the Hebrew God. It was this final thought that Shimshon and Zeponeth held dear.

Makros and his family weren't overly religious; they paid scant attention to the Philistine gods and were willing to learn more about the Hebrew beliefs and customs. All this made it easier for Shimshon to begin to plan his own future as he plotted to remove the Philistine rule over his people. He would begin by tormenting them and then, when the time was right, throw off their rule.

Shimshon looked at his future wife and thanked God for all that he had given him and was about to give him. The wedding was planned and, like all big weddings, would include a week-long feast. Finally, Shimshon felt the meaning and purpose of his life was being fulfilled. The time was now right.

Shimshon's marriage

Once again, as the family journeyed from their home to Timnah, Shimshon walked off on his own. He realised that he was again near the place where the lion attack had taken place. He remembered the strength God had given him and wondered if that strength would play a part in his tormenting of the Philistines.

Shimshon clambered over some rocks and came face to face with the carcass of the lion. Its face snarled at him in its grotesque, broken-jawed grimace. The eyes were lifeless though, as dead as at the moment God had given Shimshon the power to overcome it.

The head of the lion had been the victim of Shimshon's strength, but the body had been the victim of the circle of life. Other animals had been stripping the carcass of any meal they could find. The stomach and internal organs had all been food to some scavenger or other. Although the back of the beast was still intact, the stomach area had been ripped away. The chest had also been torn apart and it was only the ribcage that held the animal's skin in place.

A noise startled Shimshon. It was a buzzing sound, but before he could realise what it was, he felt some pain where his arm had been on the ground. He lifted the arm and saw the half-crushed, but vengeful insect hanging there. The bee had stung Shimshon and was dying, yet still the buzzing noise continued.

Shimshon followed the direction of sound and then saw where it was coming from. Inside the rotted carcass of the lion was a swarm of bees. They had made a nest there and were developing quite a community. He moved closer, while making sure he didn't rest on any other little stingers.

The smells of the countryside permeated the air but now there was an additional smell. He reached into the carcass of the dead beast and grabbed hold of the honeycomb and pulled a large lump free. He got up quickly and darted away down toward the valley floor. The bees were too slow and Shimshon too quick. He escaped with the honeycomb and the only sting he had obtained was the one when he'd leant on a bee.

The honey was delicious and Shimshon enjoyed the sweet snack as he caught up with his parent's party. Manoah and Zeponeth accepted the offered treat from their son and the journey became even more celebratory. Shimshon didn't tell anyone where the honey had come from, but he began to think about a bit of fun he could have at the wedding feast.

* * *

For a young man, the thought of a good meal would often be the highlight of a day. For Shimshon this good feeling was being multiplied on so many levels it was almost too much to take.

Manoah had gone to make further preparations, or perhaps some further business deals with Makros and his companions. And Zeponeth was with all the other women.

Shimshon was left with his thoughts and they were very pleasant indeed. He was about to start not just a pleasant meal but a pleasant week of meals. The seven-day-long feast was a highlight of any marriage. And that was another reason to be happy. Shimshon was about to be married. That was enough to bring a smile to any man's face. Especially as his bride, Ba'alshada, was an amazing woman, even if she was a Philistine.

And that was the third reason Shimshon was going to enjoy himself. The feast would give him an opportunity to begin to torment and toy with the Philistines.

* * *

Shimshon didn't have any real friends, but as part of the feast celebrations a group of thirty locals became his companions for the week. Together they would celebrate and be his 'friends'. Shimshon welcomed them to his wedding and began the fun.

'Would you like to add a little spice to this week?' Shimshon asked the group of men. They looked confused, wondering what the Hebrew was on about. 'What about a little wager, a test of your Philistine intelligence against mine, a lowly Hebrew.'

The companions drew closer to each other and discussed what Shimshon had said. The Hebrew smiled as he saw them talk amongst themselves. If they declined they would be taunted for letting this Hebrew get the better of them; however, they were wary about what exactly Shimshon wanted from them.

'What sort of wager do you have in mind?'

Shimshon smiled at the wariness of the Philistines. 'It's alright, I'm sure a people as rich as you would have no trouble paying out... if you lose. But all you have to do to win is answer a riddle.' The companions motioned for Shimshon to continue. 'If you can answer my riddle by the end of this feast I will give you each a full set of clothes.' The eyes of the companions widened in anticipation. The gift of a full set of clothes was something each of them would appreciate.

'And if we can't answer your riddle?'

Shimshon smiled back at them. 'That's easy; if you can't answer my riddle, then each of you gives me a full set of clothes.' The companions drew back to discuss the wager. Each of them would only lose one set of clothes, if they didn't win, but the Hebrew would lose thirty. There was no choice really.

'Okay, we accept. What is your riddle? Tell it to us!'

Shimshon settled back into his pile of cushions. He had been planning this since the journey to Timnah for the wedding. He knew that the Philistines wouldn't be able to answer the riddle. They would be humiliated and he would also make a tidy profit from the clothes he could sell. He cleared his throat and began the riddle.

'Out of the eater, something to eat; out of the strong, something sweet.' Shimshon smiled at them and picked up an apple. He bit into it and relished the taste of victory.

The companions settled down to begin the feast and Shimshon could see from their faces that they were confused and perhaps a little worried. The next seven days would be interesting.

★ ★ ★

'This is getting ridiculous, we have no idea what the Hebrew is on about.' Two of the companions were huddled together and they were not happy. Every group of people has its unsavoury characters and out of the thirty companions these two fitted that bill.

The companions had had no luck at all in trying to work out Shimshon's riddle, and now they were beginning to panic. For four days they had been unable to solve the question, and there were no fresh ideas coming forward from the group. They didn't want to pay out to Shimshon and these two in particular would do anything to save their money and name. And so they went to see Ba'alshada. It was time to set things right.

Ba'alshada met the two companions in private after they had asked to talk to her at the feast. She could tell they were agitated and she had a pretty good idea what the problem was. The whole wedding entourage were talking about the wager and the riddle and there was a lot of enmity building up toward Shimshon.

'This has gone far enough; it is time for us to show this Hebrew that he can't beat us. The Philistines are stronger and cleverer than the Hebrews. That is why we are ruling them. If we can't solve this riddle we will be a laughing stock.' The words came from Ekron. He was a distant cousin to Ba'alshada, but he had more connections with bandits than her family, if the rumours were right.

'If we are cleverer than the Hebrews then why can't you solve the riddle?' Ba'alshada responded, before she had thought things through. Ekron and the other companions had been drinking since the feast began and desperation was setting in. And now she had insulted Ekron in front of his friend.

'You fool. You have been taken in by his deceit and have been blinded by love. He has not given any ordinary riddle. It is a trick – something none of us could find the answer to because there is none.' Ekron was failing to keep his anger in check, although it may have had something to do with his inability to focus due to the wine.

'Then what do you want me to do?' Ba'alshada thought it best to try and placate Ekron. She was unsure what he was capable of in this state.

'Your loyalty should be with your people, not this alien,' Ekron continued. 'So, you should find out what this trick of a riddle means and tell us. Then we can win the wager, take what is ours and show that the Philistines are better than the Hebrews. Remember who you are, Ba'alshada. You are no Hebrew, and even in marriage, you are still one of us.'

Ekron's words stung Ba'alshada, but they also rang true. She would always be a Philistine, no matter how many of Shimshon's customs she followed. She was also wary of Ekron. He had a bad reputation and she didn't want there to be any trouble. Shimshon, she could tell, was also hot-headed and determined. She was worried that things could get out of hand quickly.

'I'll see what I can find out, but if it is a trick, then I may not be able to help you.' Ba'alshada tried to remain calm, but the fear could be heard in her voice. Ekron heard this and made his move.

'Oh, you'd better find out from your husband the explanation of the riddle,' Ekron moved closer and spoke quietly and directly to Ba'alshada, 'or you and all your family will pay; we'll burn you all to death. We were not invited here to be robbed.' Ekron stepped back and saw that his words had shaken Ba'alshada. He turned and went back to the feast in the knowledge of a job well done.

* * *

It was the constant drip, drip, drip from Ba'alshada that began to irritate Shimshon. He was already thinking that a life with her would not be the pleasant, peaceful perfection he had imagined. For almost seven days now, she had been asking about the riddle he had set.

At first it had just seemed like curiosity – she had simply been asking what it meant and making guesses herself. But like the thirty companions, she had not been able to get close to the answer.

Then, about halfway through the celebrations, things had changed. She had become more insistent and agitated as Shimshon had refused to tell her the riddle's meaning. She continued to try and solve it herself but still to no avail. It was also at about this time she began to use emotional blackmail on him.

Ba'alshada began to accuse him of not really loving her and of hating her. She also began to talk about 'her people' and how he hadn't given her, his wife, the answer. The implications followed. If he loved her, why hadn't he told her the answer? She was his wife; surely she should know the meaning of the riddle.

It was all becoming too much for Shimshon to take as, day after day, she threw herself on him and demanded the answer to the riddle. It was the topic of all their conversations and the hidden agenda of every meeting.

'But I haven't even told my own father and mother. They are my own people, if you want to play the race issue. Why would I tell you, a Philistine, if I haven't even told my parents?' snapped Shimshon. Ba'alshada stood there, her eyes wide open. Slowly, they filled with tears. She began to shake as Shimshon's words hit home. She shrieked and ran from the room crying and wailing at the remarks from her husband.

Shimshon had lost his temper. He hadn't meant to say those things. She had been nagging him for hours about 'her people this' and 'her people that'. It was too much for him to take and he had finally snapped. Surely he was in the right. A wife should not talk to her husband in such a way. His anger burned, but his guilt rose.

Shimshon sighed. He would have to make things right.

* * *

The celebration feast had not been a success. The food had been wonderful, the bride and groom beautiful and handsome in their own right. But the meeting of the two cultures had left a bitter taste in too many mouths.

The tension that had grown during the week because of Shimshon's riddle and wager had permeated to everyone else, not just the groom's companions. As the feast headed to its conclusion, they were still none the wiser as to the meaning of the riddle.

Shimshon needed to try and sort things out; Ba'alshada could still be heard crying in her room. She had been there since his angry outburst and had refused anyone entry. Perhaps Shimshon should share the meaning with her. The marriage meant that she was no longer just a Philistine. She would become part of his family, his race and his people.

She was only being persistent, thought Shimshon as he went to her room. Before the celebration was over he would sort things out with his wife. He would explain the riddle to her and, even if the feast hadn't been a success with the Philistines, it would at least end peacefully between himself and Ba'alshada.

★ ★ ★

The Philistine companions were at the final meal of the feast. It was just before sunset on the seventh day and the moment for settling the wager had arrived.

Shimshon sat quietly confident. He knew these men from Philistine had not been able to find the answer to the riddle. Throughout the week their attempts at answering it had been wide of the mark, and now the wager was to be settled. Shimshon would be taking tribute from the Philistines. The tide was turning.

He had also sorted things out with Ba'alshada. When he had explained the riddle to her she had visibly relaxed. She had thanked him for confiding in her and said that she and her family would always be grateful to him. Shimshon hadn't understood that, but he was more concerned with seeing these Philistines humiliated than examining every phrase spoken.

Ekron had become a natural leader to the men of the town who had been Shimshon's companions this week and it was he who stood to speak to Shimshon now. The look in his eyes concerned Shimshon. He didn't see humility or even anger and contempt at this Hebrew who had belittled them.

Ekron cleared his throat and remembered what Ba'alshada had told him about the riddle. She had come to him as soon as Shimshon had explained it to her. And he, true to his word, told her that her family would be safe as she had remembered who her people were.

'You asked us a week ago to answer a riddle and, if we did, you would give us thirty full sets of clothes.'

Shimshon narrowed his eyes as Ekron spoke; this wasn't going according to plan.

'You said, "Out of the eater, something to eat; out of the strong, something sweet." And in response we say, what is sweeter than honey and what is stronger than a lion?' Ekron smiled at Shimshon and then looked at the other Philistines around him with a victorious smug look across his face.

Shimshon lowered his head. His braids fell forward and hung beside his face. He had been betrayed. The woman who he had married had only wanted to know the answer to the riddle to tell it to Ekron and the other Philistines. They had been asking her to find out the answer from him.

Shimshon muttered to himself, 'If you had not ploughed with my heifer, you would not have solved my riddle.' They had used his wife to humiliate him and now he would have to honour the wager. Shimshon's hands were fists and he stood up, glaring at the Philistines in front of him.

He was angry beyond belief and his plan had not worked. As he stormed from the feast he prayed to Adonai to help him rid this land of these people who knew no honour and didn't serve the one true God.

★ ★ ★

It was not only anger that burned within Shimshon as he got away from the wedding. From deep within, or perhaps without, he felt a power. Something was surging through his body. He remembered the time he had confronted the group of Philistine youths all those years ago and realised that this was the same feeling, only more so.

Before he knew it, hours had passed and he wasn't sure where he was. A quick glance at the stars told him approximately where he was and the light from the moon would light his journey. He needed to honour the wager that he had made. It was important that he held his side of the deal – that was the just thing to do. But how he upheld it was another matter. It was time to clear up the land that God had given his people.

Shimshon had a plan to find the sets of clothes he needed, but it would take a bit of time. He quickened his pace, but he felt no tiredness as the power that was surging within was relieving any fatigue he should have been feeling. The light from the moon helped Shimshon's footing as he headed to Ashkelon. Shimshon knew that in that area there had been bandits operating, and even bandits wore clothes.

★ ★ ★

The four men were sitting around a small campfire and spoke in hushed tones. Shimshon slowly made his way toward them. He found it difficult to walk quietly and slowly as the power within him was making him shake. He got close enough to hear the words of the men. They were talking about a successful robbery of a trader earlier that day. Shimshon was right. They were bandits and had no place in God's country.

At first the bandits thought a lion or some other savage animal had leapt out from the bushes to attack them, such was the ferocity of the attack. Shimshon leapt from his cover and landed just behind the nearest bandit. He grabbed the robber's head and twisted it. The noise of the snapping neck was louder than the cracking of the logs in the burning fire.

The other three bandits began to rise, but as they did, Shimshon leapt over the downed robber and reached toward the fire. He picked one of the burning logs, one end not yet alight, and swung it at the bandit to his left. The red-hot log hit the bandit in the face and his scream echoed around the countryside. His face red-raw from the fire and his nose smashed from the log, he fell head first into the campfire.

The other two bandits had stepped back and one of them now went for his dagger. The iron blade flickered in the moonlight and gave confidence to the bandit who began to move toward Shimshon. He thrust the blade at the Hebrew, but that was the only aggressive act he made. Shimshon stepped to one side and knocked the blade from the robber. He kicked at the bandit's knee.

The force of the kick bent the knee the wrong way. For the second time in the fight, the noise of bone cracking and ligaments snapping echoed around the campsite.

Shimshon crouched down and picked up the fallen blade. In one swift movement he hurled it toward the one remaining bandit, who managed to raise his hands in time to grip the embedded blade in his neck. Air and blood poured from the neck wound like a babbling brook; the windpipe and artery cleanly severed.

The final bandit fell down dead, and now the only noise was the sound of sobbing pain coming from the man with the broken knee. Shimshon removed the knife from the bandit's neck and walked over to the one still in pain. He plunged the knife into his chest, 'I think this belongs to you; here, have it back.'

Shimshon began to strip the clothes from the dead bandits. The power was still flowing through his body.

'Four down, 26 to go.'

* * *

Ekron woke with a start. Something had disturbed him while he was fast asleep. He had been drinking with some friends the previous night and his head throbbed through too much wine. The talk had been about some of Ekron's unsavoury friends who had not been seen for a day or so. He shouldn't have been worried as they often stayed away for days on end due to the nature of their business, but still Ekron had felt uneasy.

He had felt the same since the end of the wedding celebrations almost a week before. The look on the Hebrew's face when he had left the proceedings had worried Ekron. He had seen the look many times before – single-minded determination. On the wrong face, that look meant trouble.

Ekron heard the noise. It was coming from outside his house. It sounded like someone was outside, moving around and moving something around too. Ekron was not one for being afraid, but he was a little nervous. He listened intently and all of a sudden the sound died. Whoever or whatever it was had either stopped moving or had left.

He had to find out what it was. So he drew a deep breath and got out of his bed. He went to the door of his house and slowly opened it, not before picking up the staff that he kept by the side for protection and a lamp to see clearly. The door opened and Ekron looked out. There was no one there, but what he saw chilled him to the bone.

Outside his house was a pile of clothes: linen inner garments and woven cloaks and shirts. The pile was large and he realised, with growing concern, that there were about thirty sets in front of him. But what really worried him was that each piece of clothing, however large or small, was either slightly burnt or stained red. Ekron knew the red staining wasn't paint: it was blood.

He lifted the lamp and looked into the countryside to see if he could see who had left the clothes outside his house. But he could see no one. He knew exactly who had done it, but the Hebrew was nowhere to be seen.

Shimshon could see Ekron though. He saw him from behind the bush he was using for cover. The wager had been honoured and the cleansing of God's land had begun. Now he needed to plan what he would do next. He should return to his wife, but the anger he felt at her betrayal still burned deep within. He only had one other place to go, so he would return to his parent's farm. As Ekron lowered the lamp, Shimshon began his journey home.

Terms of the divorce

Zeponeth's arms barely reached round to her son's back and her head barely to his chest. But he was still her little boy and she still worried about him. As she held and hugged him now she expressed her concern about the wife that he hadn't seen since the wedding.

'She's still your wife. Whatever she did and however you feel she betrayed you, you should still try to sort things out.'

'Mother…' The words and attention of his mother were making him feel more awkward by the moment. 'OK, I'll go and see her.'

Zeponeth released her son and congratulated herself on a successful mother-son discussion. 'I'll tell Manoah; he has been so worried. I think he'll spare a goat for you to take as a gift to the family. Makros will be delighted to see you and the goat will smooth over any niggles.' She hurried from the room and Shimshon realised that for the first in ages, he didn't feel angry.

* * *

Shimshon thought about the lion's carcass as he passed by where it was, but it began to bring back memories of the riddle and so he pushed it from his mind. Today wasn't a day for grudges and anger; it was a day for forgiveness and reconciliation.

The weather was playing its part too. The sun was bright but not too hot. As Shimshon walked down the road, with the goat slung over his shoulders (it had been slaughtered and cleaned back at the farm), he felt that there was nothing wrong with the world. The wheat in the fields that he passed was almost ripe; the harvest was days away and the land was being blessed. He even thought that, by marrying a Philistine, his people could be freed from the tribute. If all the Philistines became Hebrews then there would be no problem.

Diplomacy wasn't a skill that Shimshon currently had in his toolbox, but it was one he felt he could easily acquire on a day as beautiful as this. There wasn't a cloud in the sky – well perhaps one or two on the horizon, but they were far away.

* * *

Makros stood in front of Shimshon and wouldn't let him pass. He was panicked and clearly agitated trying to bar the way of the tall Hebrew.

'I am sorry, but you can't go to her room. I was so sure that you really hated her.' Makros began to shake his head as if thinking through what had happened and reaffirming his decisions.

'What are you saying, Philistine?' Shimshon was becoming angry. This was supposed to be his father-in-law, but he was denying him entry to see his wife.

'After what she did and the way you responded. I mean you've been gone ages.' Makros looked directly at Shimshon for the first time in the conversation for a while. 'I thought you didn't want Ba'alshada as a wife.' Makros lifted his jaw in defiance. 'You left her!'

'I want to see my wife!' Shimshon began to push past Makros and the Philistine tried to hold his ground, but it was his words that stopped Shimshon and not his strength.

'She is not your wife. As is our custom she was married to one of the groom's companions.' Shimshon stopped in his tracks. He could feel the anger rising in him once more. His ideas of diplomacy drained away like water spilled in the desert. Makros tried to calm the Hebrew.

'Look, the marriage was a good business move; why not marry Ba'alshada's sister. She is very attractive.'

Shimshon knocked Makros over with one flick of his arm. 'Your people have wronged me and my kind for the last time. Now I have a right to get even with you. Now I will really harm you.'

Makros watched Shimshon leave, the dust billowing after him as he strode into the distance.

'Oh Dagon, what have I done?' But there was no reply to Makros' prayer.

★ ★ ★

Shimshon had a plan but it would need to be handled with military precision, and perhaps a little divine assistance. Harvest time was near and the Philistine's fields were looking healthy. If everything continued as it had done, then a bumper crop would be harvested. But all wasn't going to go well.

As harvest drew near, so the animal life in the land increased. Shimshon's time on his father's farm wasn't a complete waste of time, even though he had begrudged every moment of it. He knew where this animal life could be found, having had to deal with it for all those years.

And now Shimshon had a plan; he would wreck the farms of all those around where he was, including Makros and the companions at his wedding. For the next few days and nights he would decimate the Philistines' harvest. There was no room for diplomacy now.

★ ★ ★

In the twilight the animal darted this way then that; its instinct driving it onward, searching for the food to live. It knew that this was the time of plenty. It knew that it would not go hungry for a while. But it also knew that these were dangerous times. Other creatures would be around and they often meant danger. It slipped through a gap in the bushes and then began to fly into the air.

Shimshon held the fox by the scruff of the neck, making sure it couldn't turn its head to bite his hand. He had been doing this for days now. He knew exactly where the foxes were; years of working on his father's farm had taught him that.

The fox gazed at Shimshon's face. 'I'm sorry little one, but I need you and it isn't going to be pleasant.' Shimshon had battled with the implications of his plan, but his anger and need for revenge was in control. At one level he knew that what he was doing was cruel, but the Philistines needed to be punished and that was what he was going to do. He seemed to have forgotten that his role was to set God's people free and not one of exacting justice.

Shimshon carried the fox along the edge of the field. Ahead of him was a sack. It rippled and writhed, like a headless and limbless body. When he reached the sack he undid it and lifted the opening in the air. The contents of the sack fell to the bottom and he thrust the fox he was carrying into the dark opening. The other foxes snapped and barked at the newcomer and then each other. The smell from inside hit Shimshon's nose and made his eyes water.

'Not long now, my little ones. But then perhaps you'll wish you were still in the sack.'

Shimshon got a small fire going as the sun finally set. He was at the edge of the field which was ripe for harvest, but it wouldn't be for long. Once again he undid the sack. He had six foxes inside and as he had done each night previously he moved with speed. He couldn't take his time on this sort of operation. He pulled first one fox, and then another, and held them down with just one huge hand. With the other, he wrapped their tails together with twine. When they were secured, he looped the twine to make a knot. The animals were now fastened by the tails. With a smooth movement Shimshon reached into the fire and pulled out a lit torch.

As the foxes barked at Shimshon and each other, but still held by his hand, he forced the torch between their bound tails until it was jammed in, it wouldn't fall out now. Then picking the foxes up, he threw them into the field. Their barks became screeches as the flame followed them through the air.

He repeated the process with the other four foxes in the sack. He did this several times each night and had been doing it for several nights now. But as the sounds of the foxes screaming reached his ears he began to wonder whether what he was doing was right.

'My Lord, what am I doing?'

* * *

Makros had heard rumours which he hadn't quite believed, but when one of the farmhands came running into the room and declared the vineyards on fire, the reality hit home. He grabbed his staff and headed out to see the problem with his precious harvest.

The fields were ablaze. Farmhands were rushing to the well and filling buckets with water, but it was clear that any effect they would have would be minimal. Tears were rolling down the face of Makros and dripping onto his cloak. There was so much water rolling down his face that the intense heat from the fields couldn't evaporate the tears before they left his face.

He tried to ask the inevitable questions of how and why, but the words never made it from his throat. He simply stared and shook his head. The farmhands did their best with the water and by beating at the fire with their cloaks but Makros could tell that the crop was lost.

As one of the farmhands beat the edge of the fire, Makros saw something move. At first he couldn't see what it was as the flames were engulfing the movement. Then he saw exactly what was moving. Makros raised his hands to his mouth in shock.

Two foxes had darted from the field. This wasn't a strange sight since foxes were common especially at the grain harvest time, which it was. What was strange was that they appeared to be connected. It was as if they had been tied together. The shock was amplified as Makros realised that their tails were on fire. Having come from the burning field this wasn't too much of a surprise, but attached to their tails was a crude torch made from kindling.

One of the foxes dropped dead and the other was stopped in its tracks. Now Makros could see that the foxes were connected at the tails, where the torch was also attached. The still-living fox tried to escape but the connection held it firm. The burning torch had burnt the tail of the fox to the flesh and was now cooking the animal alive. The fur on the back end of the animal was singed badly and the fox yelped in pain.

Makros grabbed the knife from his belt and ran to the burning animal. With a swift movement to the fox's throat he put it out of its misery. He fell to his knees and let his head drop into his hands. The fields continued to burn and slowly and surely Makros realised he was ruined.

★ ★ ★

The centre of Timnah looked like a slaughterhouse, but there would be no food from the pile of animals that was growing. Yet another farmer from the region arrived with a small cart. The donkey pulling it stopped in front of the pile of animals and tried to step back as the stench reached its muzzle.

The farmer went to the back of the cart and pulled out a burnt carcass. He walked to the pile of animals and added what was in his hands. He repeated the action a further seven times. His were the last eight burnt foxes to be brought to town.

The Philistines whose farms had been destroyed all stood looking at the pile of animals. Most were wheat farmers, but there were also vineyard and olive grove owners too, including Makros, who had called the other farmers to bring the foxes here, to Timnah.

Despite some rumours, no one knew who had done such a despicable act. Makros still couldn't believe that someone could tie the animals together and then tie a lit torch to their tails. And the scale of it was mind-blowing too. There were about 300 foxes in the pile and over 30 farms had been attacked. All this had happened over a period of several days. Now they needed answers; they wanted to know who had done this.

Ekron walked to the pile of animals and then turned to face the group of farmers. His own small farm had been one of those targeted, but he hadn't been in his house when the fire had started. He had been with a couple of his 'friends' and was returning to the farm when he had seen movement. Within minutes his field was on fire, but he didn't rush to put the fire out, because he also saw a figure emerging from the fields and slinking away into the surrounding countryside. The person's face was clearly in sight as he was carrying a lit torch with him.

'If you know something of who did this, then let us know,' said one of the olive farmers. Makros looked uneasy as the question was voiced. He had a deep fear and he hoped to Dagon that it wasn't realised. But his heart dropped as Ekron turned to face Makros.

'It was Shimshon.' Some of the farmers were ignorant as to who the person named was, while others began to turn toward Makros.

'It was Shimshon, the Hebrew.' Ekron pointed to Makros, 'The Timnite's son-in-law.' The town centre became even more silent as every eye turned to Makros. 'He did it because Makros gave his wife to another when the Hebrew left the wedding.'

Ekron hadn't come to the town meeting on his own. Several of the bandit friends who he kept close ties with were also there. Once Ekron had seen that it was Shimshon who had done this to the Philistine farmers, he contacted the bandits and told them too. He also told them that it was Shimshon who had killed the other bandits all those months before.

'You have brought this upon us,' Ekron pointed at Makros, 'you and your stupid plans to join with the Hebrew farmer.'

Makros began to argue back, but he was grabbed and held by a couple of Ekron's friends. Meanwhile, others were driving stakes into the ground next to the pile of dead foxes.

'What are you doing? Let me go!' But Makros' words had no effect on those holding him.

'Your stupid plans and your stupid daughter.' Ekron looked across the road and saw more of his cronies arriving and they weren't alone. Between them they were dragging Ba'alshada kicking and screaming.

Both Makros and Ba'alshada were brought to where the stakes had been driven into the ground and they were tied to them and each other. And then they watched as small logs of wood and kindling were brought and placed around them. Their screams and cries for mercy fell on death ears.

Ekron brought a lit torch from one of the trading houses over to the tied-up father and daughter.

'You brought this on us; you have destroyed our harvest and so we will destroy you. Then we'll go and find that coward of a Hebrew and tear him apart.'

'Please Ekron, don't do this, we are as much victims as you are. My vineyard has been destroyed too.'

'Then you shall die like the other victims of Shimshon, the foxes.'

Ekron dropped the torch into the kindling around the Tishbite and his daughter. Like the foxes before, Makros and Ba'alshada screamed as the flames took hold. Makros turned to look at his daughter and saw the terror in her eyes. He was sure she could see the same reflected in his. At first there was nothing to feel, but then the heat began. Makros thought it strange that the first parts of his body that felt warm were his shins and not his feet, but as he looked he realised that this was because it was where the flames began to lick. But this was the last coherent thought he had as the pain began to spread up his body. His cloak was alight now and Ba'alshada's too. They cried out to Dagon for help but then simply screamed in pain. Their screams were never quite engulfed by the roar of the fire until they died.

Ekron called the farmers and the bandits together and with one voice they roared their revenge.

'Now for the Hebrew.'

★ ★ ★

Shimshon had been hiding nearby when he saw the plume of smoke rising from Timnah. He finished the fruit he had been eating and set off toward the town. For the past few days, he had been the one setting off the fires, so he was curious as to where this smoke was coming from.

As he entered the town he heard a loud roar from the centre and he slowed his approach. It sounded like there were a lot of angry people ahead. His body began to tingle again with the power that had helped him overcome the bandits and he immediately began to have a bad feeling about what was happening.

He stopped when the centre came into view. He could see a crowd of men and in front of them, Ekron. They were all looking in the same direction, toward the smoke. Shimshon stepped a little closer and steered himself so he could see between the men to the base of the rising cloud. He stopped, looked and closed his eyes in shame.

Two burnt bodies were tied to the ground; the wood that had been their funeral pyre was exhausted and now smouldered around them. From the faces he recognised in the crowd and the words that carried to where he stood, he realised that the bodies belonged to Makros and Ba'alshada. Whatever Shimshon had done in reaction to what they had done, in no way warranted the reaction of Ekron and the others.

'Now there will be revenge...'

Shimshon's voice floated across the town centre. One by one the Philistines turned around to see who had spoken the words. And one by one they readied themselves for a fight as they saw the Hebrew standing before them.

'... And I won't stop.'

Before the last of the farmers had turned around, Shimshon had felled the first and taken his scythe. The next few fell as various parts of their bodies were clinically removed by the scythe. Shimshon swung the blade and it bit deep into the neck of a farmer. As the scythe severed the artery, blood pumped several feet into the air with the rhythm of a heartbeat. The farmer's cry of pain stopped abruptly as the scythe continued its journey through the man's voice box, the scream no more than a gargled release of air from his lungs. The bones in the next man cracked like a twig. And the passage of the scythe was so fast that when it reached the artery on the other side of the neck there was still enough blood pressure to produce a second fountain. The head flew through the air as it was finally separated from the farmer's body, which slumped lifeless to the floor.

Arms, legs and more heads went flying as Shimshon charged through the crowd. Each one dispatched with ruthless efficiency and never needing more than one swing of the scythe to cut through flesh, sinew and bone. Shimshon left a bloody trail as he advanced through the crowd.

His direction wasn't random, it was direct. Those who fell were those who stood between Shimshon and his goal: Ekron. His recent nemesis realised what was happening and asked for help from his bandit friends. There was no help forthcoming from any of the farmers. As they realised where Shimshon was heading, they began to clear a path for him.

Two of the bandits moved between Shimshon and his prey. The first had a large piece of wood in his hands. It looked like it had come from the fire as one end was blackened. He positioned himself in front of Shimshon who swung the scythe through the air in an arc. The bandit raised the wood with both hands and the scythe's blade embedded itself. With the bandit still holding onto the wood Shimshon pulled the scythe back towards himself. The bandit came flying toward Shimshon, who let go of the scythe and headbutted the bandit as he arrived through the momentum of the pull. The bandit's skull fractured with the force of Shimshon's blow and he dropped down to the floor. Moments later, straw-coloured liquid began to flow from the bandit's ear.

The last bandit had a short sword and Shimshon had nothing to protect himself. The bandit took his chance and charged at the defenceless Hebrew. He would run the Hebrew through with his sword and end this carnage. As he ran, Shimshon threw the lifeless body of the previous bandit through the air. The body hit the bandit, crashing into him and stopping his charge. The bandit fell to the ground dropping the sword from his hand. Shimshon leant over, picked up the sword and pinned the bandit to the ground by plunging it through his stomach.

Ekron stood before Shimshon. There was nowhere for him to run.

'We had to do it; it was because of them that our lives have been ruined. Our crops destroyed and our livelihoods gone.' Shimshon wasn't listening, he simply walked toward Ekron.

'Wait, what are you going to do? Hey wait, put me down!'

Shimshon lifted the Philistine like he was weightless and held him above his head. He then took him to the smouldering remains of the fire. As he approached, he could feel the heat still rising. The flames may have died down but the wood was still red-hot.

It was onto this that Shimshon put Ekron and held him there by placing his foot on his chest. Ekron screamed in agony as the heat of the wood spread through his body. The Philistine could feel his back erupting in blisters and the pain was intense. Thankfully, the pain didn't last long as the heat burnt through all the nerves in his back.

His clothes began to smoke and then they ignited. Once more the centre of the town was filled with the scream of someone burning to death. Shimshon held Ekron on the fire until he stopped fighting and within minutes the Philistine was dead.

The rest of the farmers had scattered as Shimshon had focused on Ekron and now Shimshon needed to get away too. He knew it wouldn't be long until news reached the Philistine militia and a different fight would begin. He left the town and headed toward Etam. He knew there was a cave there that he could hide in. But that wouldn't help for long – he needed another plan.

Settlement

Years before, a young boy had dreamed of being a mighty warrior like his father. Now, he too wore the armour and a feathered helmet. At his side was a sheathed sword. He had been taught well by his father and if all went well and Dagon blessed him, he would follow his father as Captain of the Guard when he stood down.

He looked at his father and just for a moment, he noticed a look in his eye. The last time he had seen that look was over ten harvest seasons ago. The young boy and his father had gone into the courtyard outside their house to do some sword practice. But unlike other times, this was an excuse to leave the house, rather than to teach his son how to fight.

The soldier's wife, the boy's mother, had been unwell and had been getting worse. The soldier could face anything – he had stood up against many enemies, but he couldn't face what was to happen. Their practice had been half-hearted and when the servant came from the house and stood in front of the soldier with his head bowed, the boy saw the look.

He couldn't describe it, but he had a good idea what it meant; fear of the unknown. His father was about to face an unknown future. His wife was dead and now Abbad'agon had to go ahead with life, and he had no idea where it would go.

Shennahgon wondered what his father was thinking; why was he unsure of the future?

* * *

Abbad'agon felt uneasy. There was something about this situation that left him feeling everything was not quite as it seemed. And what was more worrying was that he thought his son could see the look in his eye too.

Abbad'agon had gone to the temple that morning and sought guidance from the seers there. The priest had pulled one of the chickens from the cage, once Abbad'agon had paid the required offering to Dagon, and held it over the cutting stone. The prayer for divination had been uttered and the sacrifice took place.

The priest raised a jewelled dagger into the air and slit the chicken from below the beak through the breast and to the bird's rear. Then with a quick movement the entrails of the dead, but still warm hen, were pulled across the cutting stone.

His bony fingers splayed the gut, liver and intestines. He prodded and poked and uttered unintelligible incantations. He reached into a pocket of his priestly robes and threw some fine dust into the flaming bowl that lay next to the cutting stone. A plume of coloured smoke rose into the air, accompanied by more unknown words.

Abbad'agon waited for the ritual to end and for the omens to be revealed.

'Abbad'agon, Captain of the Seranim's guard, Dagon and the gods are with you this day. Once again our lord, Dagon, will be shown as powerful.' Again the priest reached into his robe and threw more powder onto the flame.

'This day will bring another victory to our mighty god and his army.' The coloured smoke began to puff into the air as before, but this time a gust of wind entered the temple, and before the plume reached its zenith, the smoke was dispersed and the fire itself extinguished.

The priest looked at the bowl in surprise and then shrugged his shoulders.

'Well, that was strange. I've never seen that happen before. Abbad'agon, Captain of the Guard, would you like another reading of your glorious future? I'm sure Dagon would accept a reduced offering seeing you've already been so generous.'

The priest's words faded as Abbad'agon walked from the temple. The divination may have shown victory, but the extinguishing of the flame was an omen that Abbad'agon was concerned about. What did that mean?

★ ★ ★

The camp was set up quickly and, after some discussion with the survivors of the events in Timnah, Abbad'agon sent out search parties around Lehi to look for the Hebrew. He had been shocked at the violence that the Hebrew had displayed. But he was even more shocked at the power and ease with which he had been able to do what he did.

From all the accounts that Abbad'agon had heard, the Hebrew had displayed superhuman strength and power. Although he thought that much of what was being relayed to him had been exaggerated, it was clear that Shimshon was more powerful than anyone he had heard about.

With the feeling of unease he had carried since the divination episode at the temple, Abbad'agon knew he would have to handle this one carefully. There were things at play here that he didn't understand. If only he could make things a little easier – somehow change the situation and the odds.

Abbad'agon prayed to Dagon for advice and for his god to send some help.

'Father!' It was Shennahgon. 'There is a Hebrew delegation here; they want to know what we are here for and how they may assist us.'

Abbad'agon thanked Dagon for a swift answer to prayer.

★ ★ ★

Yeshua approached Abbad'agon with all the timidity of a mouse trying to pass a sleeping cat. He didn't want to be anywhere near the Philistine army captain, let alone talk to him. The Philistines were technically ruling the Hebrews but it was a give-and-take relationship. The Hebrews paid the Philistines a tribute and the Philistines looked after the Hebrews. Or that was how it worked in theory.

It was Yeshua's duty, under the terms of the tribute, to find out what the Philistines wanted... and then to help them. It was like rubbing salt into an open wound. To compound the issue, Yeshua had heard the rumours about Shimshon. This could potentially become a very volatile situation.

Yeshua bowed before Abbad'agon despite every fibre in his body crying out against it. What was required was not necessarily what was right, and Yeshua longed for the time when Israel would not be ruled by others. But this situation was worrying and he didn't know how this meeting would go.

'Captain, you bring a great and mighty army to our land. Have you come to fight us?' Yeshua followed the traditional rules for dealing with their Philistine rulers.

'Because you have come to see us, then we may not need to fight.' Yeshua remained prostrate in front of Abbad'agon as he spoke.

'You are aware of the problem in Timnah?' The Hebrew captain nodded from his bowed position.

'Good, then I'll make you a proposal.' Abbad'agon began to walk around Yeshua as he continued. 'We have come to take Shimshon prisoner. He must be punished for what he has done. We will do to him what he has done to us.'

Abbad'agon had circled Yeshua and was now back in front of him.

'We don't want to march through your land and take Shimshon from it as it's possible that would cause unrest and we may need to enforce our rule. However, if you could go and find Shimshon, and bring him to us, we can go back to Gaza, leaving you in peace.'

Yeshua thought deeply about what he was being asked to do, but the answer was obvious – he had to protect his people and if one man had to die to save others, then so be it.

'I'll take my men and find Shimshon. When we have him, I'll send notice and you can collect him from us.'

'Good.' Abbad'agon turned and left. Yeshua rose when the Captain was gone and with a heavy heart set off to find Shimshon.

* * *

When Yeshua and the Judah militia got to Etam, it didn't take them long to find out where Shimshon was. They had little trouble in persuading the locals that they weren't there to cause any trouble but needed to speak to Shimshon. A couple of boys had seen Shimshon up in the local caves, and Yeshua knew that was a good place to hide.

Yeshua took a couple of trusted men into the hills for the short climb to the cave where Shimshon had been seen. It wouldn't take them long to reach it. On the journey Yeshua thought about what had happened and what it could all mean in Adonai's plan.

Yeshua feared the Lord, followed the Law of Moses and prayed each day. For a military man, he knew where the real power and strength lay. He also knew that, as a people, they were being punished by God for not staying true to him. They had forgotten the law, forgotten that this land had been given to them by God and because of that the land had been taken back from them.

But was God doing something new here? Had he raised Shimshon to fight the Philistines? Was Shimshon another Gideon? The Hebrew army were many, but they lacked a leader and a standard bearer, someone who could rally the troops and restore their honour and their faith in God, someone to show them that the Lord cared for them and was on their side.

All these thoughts were going through his head as he climbed. When they got to the entrance of the cave, Yeshua and the men stopped. One of the locals had told them that the caves extended deep into the hills and it was very easy to get lost, or hide, in them.

'Shimshon! Shimshon, are you in there?' Yeshua's question echoed into the mouth of the cave but returned unanswered. 'Shimshon, my name is Yeshua. I lead the Judean militia. I want to talk to you.' Again there was no answer. Yeshua looked at the other soldiers with him, but they merely shrugged back.

'Shimshon, don't you realise what you've done? The Philistines are rulers over us; they want justice and they want revenge. Do you not care about your people? They will punish us if they can't get to you. What have you done to your people?'

Yeshua's pleas managed a response from a bird that flew out from the cave, a couple of small grubs in its beak, ready for expectant mouths in its nest.

'We've come to take you to them. They want us to tie you up and hand you over.' Yeshua thought the truth was the best way to get a response from Shimshon, and it did, though not the one he expected.

'Yeshua, that's a fine name, with a fine tradition.' Yeshua tried to see where the voice was coming from, but he couldn't. The other members of his squad were doing the same and getting the same result, although they weren't moving any closer; Shimshon's reputation had preceded him.

'The Lord saves.' Shimshon let the words hang there on their own. 'The Philistines are cowards; they know no honour. They don't have a god of justice, so they know no justice.'

Yeshua felt Shimshon was talking to them, but he wasn't sure since the words were stated so matter-of-factly.

'They killed my wife and my father-in-law. I merely did to them what they did to me.' Again Yeshua wasn't sure whether Shimshon was justifying his actions or making a case to the Judean militia to let him go.

'Shimshon, they want us to take you to them.'

For the first time Yeshua got a direct response from Shimshon. 'They sent you to get me and tie me up; they are scared of what I could do.'

Yeshua and the others in his group stepped back. They too had heard what Shimshon could do and were scared. And it seemed Shimshon had sensed this. 'Promise me that you won't kill me yourselves.'

Yeshua turned to the others around him and they hastily nodded.

'We promise we will not kill you. I promise in the sight of our God.' Yeshua looked into the darkness of the entrance of the cave. The total lack of light offered no glimpse of the one they were looking for. Then, as if it were smoke solidifying, a figure formed. The larger-than-life form of Shimshon stepped from the blackness of the cave.

He stood before Yeshua and smiled.

'The Lord saves.' He held out his hands, the wrists held tightly together, offering then to be bound.

'We won't kill you; we'll only tie you up. Then we'll hand you over to the Philistines.' Yeshua took some rope from one of the other soldiers and began to tie up Shimshon's arms. As he did so he smiled at the man before him.

'Yes, Yahweh saves.'

The soldiers led Shimshon down the hill and then up toward where the Philistines waited.

★ ★ ★

'Shennahgon!' Abbad'agon called his son. It was time to make some decisions and issue some orders.

'We'll saddle up and march to meet the Judean militia. I don't want to give them time to make any plans of their own. I'll lead our men and you can ride at the rear – that way we'll be able to control all our men, with me at one end, and you at the other.' What Abbad'agon wasn't telling his son was his concern. Although the idea sounded plausible, he really wanted his son away from any danger while he assessed the situation.

'We march immediately – let's go and dispense some Philistine justice.' Abbad'agon clapped his son on the back as he left the tent and went to saddle up his horse. He was already beginning to think the omen was nothing more than coincidence.

★ ★ ★

Shimshon, though bound with brand new rope, led the Judean militia. His lone figure was at the head of the marching troop. Behind him were two soldiers who half-heartedly held spears in case of any problems.

Behind them walked Yeshua, who was praying as he walked. And behind him were 3,000 men, the whole Judean militia. Yeshua wasn't sure what was going to happen. They had bound Shimshon and then Shimshon had asked to walk in front of the militia as they took him to the Philistine camp.

All he could do was pray and trust in Adonai. God had promised that he would be with his people if they trusted and obeyed him. Yeshua knew that they had failed, but he also knew that Adonai was just and that if they trusted again, he would once again be with them.

He knew Shimshon had been brought up a Nazirite, one who had been set aside to do God's work. Could he be the one who would free them from the rule of the Philistines?

Slowly and surely Shimshon began to feel the power rise in his body again. The tingling was there, the sensation was there and the Spirit of Adonai was there. Behind him he could feel the presence of the Judean militia, but he knew that today was all about God's power.

The road they walked on curved, and a valley came into view. The valley was narrow and Shimshon realised that any Philistine army would have to squeeze into a narrow column to get through. As he watched, a Philistine soldier on horseback came into view, leading a narrow snake of men through the valley.

Shimshon had a momentary flashback, to the image the old priest had drawn in the sand. It was a valley and there were stick people drawn in the valley. He realised that this was what the old priest had drawn. The Philistine army had come to meet Shimshon and take him, but to do that they had come through the valley. And now they were strung out and vulnerable.

Abbad'agon had entered the valley thinking that the Judeans were still a way off. He knew they weren't as disciplined as his men and wouldn't be marching as fast or as organised. So when he saw the muscular Hebrew, the two guards and then the rest of the Judean army come into view, it took him momentarily by surprise.

He looked back at his own army which were spread out and stuck in the valley. This was not the best place to fight. If the Judeans were able to get on either side of the valley his army would be out-flanked.

Abbad'agon had to think fast and take back the initiative. Hopefully the Judeans would be as surprised as he was at seeing the other army. If he could confuse them, then he may turn this into his advantage.

He turned round to the horn blower behind him, 'Sound the attack.'

The horn blasted its sound down the valley and the Philistine army roared and began to move forward with determination and more speed.

Shimshon heard the trumpet blast and the tingling inside his body grew. All at once he knew this was it. This was the time he had been waiting for. This was the moment his life had been heading for. This was God's time to free the Hebrews from the rule of the Philistines

At the side of the road was the body of a recently deceased animal. Shimshon ran toward it and realised it was a donkey. He remembered the donkey from his parents' farm and the journeys they had taken together to trade his father's grain.

The power-tingling rose like a wave readying itself to come crashing down onto the beach. As it did, the rope that had held him tight began to loosen, as if it had turned from being newly-made into old, frayed and burnt pieces of binding.

Shimshon flexed his muscles and the rope fell from his arms – he was free and almost ready. He reached down to the head of the donkey and pulled it apart in a similar way that he had pulled apart the head of the lion. Once again the jaw broke from the rest of the skull. But this time Shimshon pulled it completely free.

He stripped the skin and dead flesh from the bone. The jaw was made up of two bones and he discarded one and held the other like a club. It wasn't the most sophisticated weapon, but with Adonai on his side, it would be effective.

Shimshon leapt from the dead animal and began to run toward the valley, leaving behind the rest of the stunned Judean army. He answered the roar of the Philistines with one of his own and entered the narrow valley, using the sloped valley wall to gain some height as he approached the first of the Philistines. This man was obviously their leader as he was the only one on horseback that he could see.

Abbad'agon had to face the Hebrew charging toward him, but he didn't want to be too exposed and alone, so he hadn't charged on his horse to meet him. As the

Hebrew had entered the valley Abbad'agon saw he had some sort of weapon in his hand.

He drew his own sword and prepared to do battle, the rest of his army trapped in the narrow valley. He could see the Hebrew using the valley walls to gain some height advantage and Abbad'agon began to have a really bad feeling about what would happen. At the same time it felt like a gust of wind was howling down the valley toward him.

The Hebrew was several metres away from him, but he was now above him on the valley wall, despite Abbad'agon being on the back of his horse. He raised his sword and prepared for the Hebrew's attack. It came quickly and ferociously.

Shimshon launched himself from the valley wall, jumping toward the Philistine on horseback, who lifted his sword as protection. As the space between them reduced, Shimshon swung the jawbone through the air in an arc. His speed, momentum and reach meant that the jawbone connected with the hand of the Philistine, knocking the sword away from Shimshon's chest to which it had been aimed.

As the jawbone connected with the Captain's hand, bones cracked at the force of the impact. The Philistine cried out in pain until, seconds later, Shimshon's fist cracked the Captain's jawbone. The force knocked the Philistine from his horse and he landed awkwardly on the ground, a rock becoming a makeshift pillow that cracked more bones.

Shimshon had managed to balance and remain on the horse. He turned the beast around so that he was now facing the rest of the Philistine army and he demanded that it race toward them. The horse reared up and then galloped at the stunned soldiers who had just seen their leader being swatted like a fly.

The power was still surging through Shimshon and as the horse piled into the soldiers, Shimshon swung the jawbone again. The Philistines were trapped; the valley's natural shape had come to Shimshon's aid. First one, then two, then three and four were felled by the force of the jawbone and Shimshon's swing.

The horse's momentum was slowing as the Philistines piled up, both living and dead. Then the horse reared up. A Philistine spear was embedded deep into its chest. Shimshon fell from the back of the animal, narrowly escaping the falling horse by rolling out of the way. The dead beast added to the pile of corpses filling the valley.

Shimshon picked up one of the discarded Philistine spears and threw it. One of the advancing Philistines stood still as the spear pierced through the thin armour he was wearing, such was the force of Shimshon's throw.

The spear continued its journey and the Philistine looked down to see the end of the spear disappear through the front of his chest. At first there was just a hole and, surprisingly for the Philistine, no pain. Then the hole welled up with thick red blood until it overflowed and poured from the soldier's chest. His bright shiny armour was smeared with blood, but he wouldn't worry about getting it clean. There was no pain because there was no feeling. The soldier was dead. They were lifeless eyes that were staring at the mess.

The spear emerged from the Phlistine's back and continued its journey trailing the soldier's blood, flesh and organs. The same thing happened to the two Philistines who were standing in line behind the first. Each one was first pierced and then skewered by the spear before it advanced to the next.

The spear came to a halt in the chest of another soldier, its force finally, fatally spent. Shimshon pushed the dying Philistine to one side as he continued his deadly rampage into the Philistine force. The Lord's power was still coursing through his body.

Yeshua watched at the entrance to the valley as Shimshon decimated the Philistines. Time after time he saw the jawbone swing and down another soldier. He had never seen anything like it. This was not natural.

The speed and strength of Shimshon was beyond anyone Yeshua knew and had ever heard of. He knew that this was the doing of Adonai.

He called the Judean militia to advance into the valley although he wasn't sure Shimshon needed any help. Apart from the help he was currently getting from God.

Shimshon held the head of a Philistine with one hand and then brought the jawbone crashing down right where the neck met the shoulder. The soldier immediately crumpled to the ground, his leg twitching spasmodically as the destroyed nerves lost control over the body.

He noticed the rest of the Philistines were no longer advancing toward him. Slowly, and in agreement with each other, they lowered their shields, spears and swords and placed them on the ground. They also lowered their heads in submission to the Hebrew.

Shimshon looked back along the valley, the way he had come. At one end, the Judean militia were making their way toward him, their swords raised in victory as they chanted the name of Shimshon. In between, and now under their feet, it looked like a thousand Philistine bodies lay either dead or dying.

Shimshon climbed up the valley wall so that he could get a better view of everything. The remaining Philistine army had all put down their weapons and surrendered. Some had begun to help those who hadn't been killed but were only injured.

'Tend to your dead and dying.' Shimshon told the Philistines, and slowly and warily they began to move along the valley.

Shennahgon ran fowards and slid down next to his father's fallen body. It had taken him a long time to work his way along to the far end, but he was now there. He put his arm beneath Abbad'agon's shoulder and lifted him up; he used his other hand to turn his father's face. Shennahgon looked into the broken visage of the dying Captain of the Guard.

'I will avenge you, father.'

'Wait,' Abbad'agon had found strength from somewhere deep within and although his voice rasped, the note of authority stopped Shennahgon from leaving. 'Shimshon is too strong. There are supernatural things happening here that we don't understand. Dagon has let this animal have power this day. You cannot defeat him. But one day the time will be right. Dagon will show you, and Shimshon will be handed over to us. You must take your time. Build up your army and your strength, believe in Dagon's power and make the necessary sacrifices to him, and you will be rewarded. Ask him for Shimshon and eventually he will be given to you. Trust in your god.'

The broken body of Abbad'agon shook. It took one last sharp intake of breath and the air drained from his lungs. He was gone. Shennahgon wept while he held his father in his arms.

★ ★ ★

Yeshua stood before Shimshon with the rest of the militia spread out along the valley. Shimshon jumped on a rock on the valley wall to see even further and addressed the militia of Judah.

'With a donkey's jawbone
  I have made donkeys of them.
With a donkey's jawbone
  I have killed a thousand men.'

The roar from the Judean militia filled the valley.

'The Philistine army is decimated and defeated. They have laid down their weapons and will no longer fight me or us.' Shimshon raised the jawbone above his head. 'Today is a great day, for this day is the day the Hebrews stopped paying tribute to the Philistines. This is the day that Adonai, our God, gives us back this land. The land he promised our forefathers.' Shimshon's voice somehow managed to rise above the continued roar.

'This day at Ramath Lehi, the Lord our God has given us back the land. Once again we are a free people – free to worship Adonai and no other.' This time Shimshon didn't try to speak over the noise. He let the celebrations die down of their own accord. It took some time.

He turned to the Philistines and addressed them. 'Your time as our rulers has come to an end. We have taken back our land. Now go back to your cities and stay there. Return to your little walled kingdoms and don't come back. For I'll be waiting and next time I won't kill one thousand, I'll kill ten thousand and then tens of thousands. Stay out of our land.'

Gates

Shimshon felt the passion within him again, but this was not the Spirit of the Lord. It had been years since his marriage had fallen apart. Yet he was still a man, a man with passions and desires, a man who had difficulty handling those desires, often letting them take control rather than controlling them and trying to handle them himself, instead of asking God for help.

Since his victory with the army of Judah over the Philistine militia, the tribute had been stopped. The Philistines didn't have the military power or the willpower to enforce the tax, with Shimshon at the head of the army. But Shimshon wanted more. He wanted the Philistines to know that they weren't welcome or safe in the land that Adonai had given to his people.

So Shimshon set off for Gaza, the greatest of the Philistine cities. He would show them that he could come and go whenever and wherever he wanted and they couldn't do anything to stop him. He would rub it in their faces: they were not in charge anymore.

Shimshon didn't get much further than the city gates, but it wasn't the passion of making the Philistine's pay that was controlling him. As he stood at the entrance to the great city at dusk, Shimshon let his eyes wander:

the massive gates, the traders completing their business, the drinking dens, the brothels...

The prostitute was well practised at enticing men to her room. She knew what to do – the right look, the right flash of skin, the whispered word. She'd seen the strange-looking man enter the city and knew that she could make some money. She put all her years of experience into action to attract the Hebrew, calling to him, touching the braided hair, flattering him... There was no way he could resist.

Shimshon saw the woman approach and the desires that lurked within him took control. He went with her into the inn where she worked from. But he didn't go unobserved. Guards at the gate had seen their giant enemy enter the city and go with the woman. Other prostitutes had noticed the hair and the physique. Traders had matched the stories of the leader of Israel with the man who had walked in their midst. Shimshon was in Gaza.

★ ★ ★

It was like a shower of rain. First there was one drop, then another and then several more. Where once there had been clear air, it was now full of raindrop after raindrop. Finally the shower became a torrent. It was everywhere; it soaked everything and it left nothing dry.

The rumour raced through the city.

'It was Shimshon, I tell you.'

'The one who defeated the army at Lehi.'

'He entered the inn at market street.'

'He's there now.'

'In this city with a prostitute.'

'He killed thousands with a donkey's jaw bone.'

'What are we going to do?'

'He's there now!'

The small garrison that was left included one lonely and dejected young soldier, bent on revenge. Shennahgon had buried his father and was now biding his time, just as he had been told. When the rumour reached him, he realised it was the chance he had been waiting for. He gathered the militia together and began to make his plan.

'We'll wait till morning; let him think he has got away with it,' Shennahgon told the group of soldiers. They viewed him with wary eyes. 'He'll be tired after he leaves the inn, but we won't be. We'll rest this night and wake early in the morning. He'll have had little sleep and won't be as strong as he was at Lehi.'

Reluctantly, the rest of the militia agreed to Shennahgon's plan. After all, it was a good one and made perfect sense. However, in the back of their minds they were worried. Some had been present at the massacre of Lehi and the rest had heard the stories. Shimshon was a giant who had supernatural strength.

Still, they went to their posts and settled down to sleep and rest, knowing that in the morning they would be fresh to face the Hebrew. But would that be fresh enough? None of them knew.

* * *

Shimshon woke with a start. From the open window he could see the moon high in the sky. It was the middle of the night. Was it a dream? He lifted himself onto his elbows and thought for a moment. He couldn't remember clearly… What had happened? The whole evening had been a daze. He looked at the bed and saw the woman there.

What had he been doing? Why had he come here? He vaguely remembered the yearning, the desire to be here. But he knew the danger. So why had he put himself in such a position? He had felt out of control; he had been out of control. He shook his head, trying to get some clarity, and his braids whipped around like a lion's mane.

'My Lord, forgive me, and my Lord, even though I don't deserve it, please be with me and help me.'

'He's here in Gaza. We'll get him in the morning.' The voice was as clear as any spoken, but it was in

Shimshon's head. So that was what they were going to do. His anger at their impudence was matched by his anger at his own stupidity and lack of self-control. He climbed from the bed and quickly pulled on his clothes that were laid on a chest to one side of the room. The noise made him start.

The girl in the bed stirred only to roll over and stop the snoring that had just made Shimshon jump. He needed a plan and he needed to sort things out, and so first things first.

Shimshon fell to his knees, bowed his head and began to mutter his prayer, 'Adonai, God of my salvation, forgive me. Your servant has brought shame on himself and therefore you, his Lord. Forgive me and show me a way out of this situation. And deliver into my hands these enemies who worship idols and dishonour you with their actions and oppress your people. Forgive me and restore your honour, my Lord Adonai.'

Shimshon remained on his knees listening with every fibre of his being for a response from his God. And slowly, in the quiet of this room, at the place of his sin, Shimshon felt God's forgiveness fill his being. And as Shimshon realised he had been forgiven, a plan began to form in his head and slowly he began to rise from his knees.

The brothel was silent as Shimshon slipped from his room and made his way across the area that doubled as a bar as well as a place to choose what girl you wanted. It was eerie, with no one making a noise and no girls vying for attention. Several passed-out revellers littered the floor, but apart from them, there was no one around.

The streets of Gaza were equally deserted and silent as Shimshon crept through them. He still couldn't believe that he had come here on his own into this dangerous situation, but it looked like he was going to get out safely. He kept an eye on each footfall as it would only take one noise and the whole town would awaken and come crashing down on him.

He made it to the gatehouse but the joy and relief of getting there was short-lived. The gates, he realised too late, were bolted. Shut for the night to keep bandits and thieves away. The large beam that was used to keep the gates locked was firmly in place. The gates with their wooden posts and cross bar were closed. Shimshon was trapped.

For the second time that night Shimshon lowered his head and prayed. Gaza remained silent and asleep as the man, slightly larger than the average man, and with long, braided hair, stood bowed in front of the gates. Slowly he raised his head and if anyone had been there to see, they would have noticed a huge grin erupt across his face.

Shimshom stepped forward, toward the gates. He lowered his head again, but this time it wasn't in prayer.

This time it enabled him to put his head beneath the giant locking beam of the gates. Now his shoulders were pressing on the beam. He lifted his muscled arms and stretched them out so that each arm was along the beam and each hand gripped the piece of wood. Shimshon then began to push.

★ ★ ★

Ben'agon had sneaked into the beautiful girl's room and she had been waiting for him. She poured him some wine and gave him some fruit to eat. 'My father has left on one of his trading trips and he won't be back for a week. We have the house for ourselves.'

Ben'agon smiled and took the wine and fruit, 'I know – I saw him leave earlier. I know everything there is to know in this city.' The girl reached out and stroked Ben'agon's beard and lent forward ready to kiss the gatekeeper.

'I should have known it was you!'

The girl shrieked and the wine and fruit went flying through the air. In through the door had burst a giant of a man. It was the girl's father, somehow returned from his journey. 'You don't know anything that goes on in this city. You are a fool, a fool who falls asleep far too often when he should be keeping an eye on the gates!'

The big man reached into his robe and pulled something out. 'I'll teach you a lesson for falling asleep when you should be keeping watch.' The man unfolded the whip in his hand and then lifted it over his head before flicking it forward toward Ben'agon. 'Crack!'

Ben'agon was waiting for the pain of the whip to register, but it didn't come. 'Crack!' There was the noise again, but no pain. In fact there was no giant with a whip, and no girl with wine and fruit. Ben'agon had been sleeping again. It was his responsibility to keep watch over the gate, but again he had fallen asleep on the job. At least, he wasn't going to get whipped. He settled back into the comfy pile of cushions and hoped the dream of the girl would come again, this time without the return of the father.

'Crack!' The noise brought Ben'agon to full attention. He leapt from his cushions and darted from his room beside the gates and stopped dead in his tracks. The gates were moving, they were buckling and they were cracking.

It was then that he realised what was going on – a man was pushing through the gates. The gates themselves were loosening their hinges and the posts they were attached to were being pulled from the ground. The cross bar that joined the two posts was hanging on to them like a fisherman who had fallen overboard.

With one final cracking noise, the whole structure came loose, seeming to fall apart whilst remaining in one piece. That didn't surprise Ben'agon since everything he was seeing seemed impossible. The man who had pulled the structure loose and apart was now leaving Gaza, but he wasn't leaving empty-handed.

The main locking beam was still on Shimshon's shoulders, and hanging from this beam were the two gates themselves. Dragging from the gates were the two supporting posts, now completely uprooted from the ground. Finally, attached to one of the supporting posts, was the cross bar. With super-human strength Shimshon was dragging the whole gate and heading out on the main road toward Hebron.

Ben'agon stared, unable to say or do anything. He was being joined by others too. They had been woken by the commotion and had come to the gate. And there they stopped, Shennahgon and the militia among them. Their disbelief at what they were seeing was paralysing them. All they could do was stand and stare. They knew it was Shimshon; they knew he was on his own, but they also knew exactly what this meant.

Shimshon had defeated their soldiers. He had revoked the tribute between the Philistines and the Hebrews – the deal which saw the Philistines protect the Hebrews for a payment and deference. But now the gate of Gaza had been pulled down. The symbol of their own protection had been removed. And it had been removed by a Hebrew. Shimshon had set his people free.

★ ★ ★

The weight on Shimshon's shoulders was colossal, but it wasn't slowing him down. He was heading for the hills and would drop the gates when he reached them. Shimshon also knew what the removal of the gates symbolised, but he knew that it wasn't his actions that had set his people free. It was the Hebrew's God working through him, the God of Abraham, Jacob and Joseph. The God who had rescued his people from Egypt had now released his people from the control of the Philistines. God's people were free!

PART THREE

Love unrequited?

D'lila's father gazed at his daughter. He was in the vineyard checking the vines, making sure that they were tied to their supports and not being blighted. He had glanced up and seen his daughter come out of the house to get some water from the well. Her striking features, dark, untamed hair and bright clothes stood out against the bleached walls of their home.

She was unmarried and so far there had been no acceptable suitors. Well, he and his wife had found them acceptable, but D'lila was very hard to please.

Life had been hard on the Philistines this past 20 years. Since the Hebrews had rebelled, the peace had been tense between the two peoples. Trade had continued, but beneath the surface, there was always the fear that things could escalate into war.

And things were all down to one person really, the self-made leader of the Hebrews, Shimshon. Leader? He was more a figurehead, thought Abanata, as he worried about the world his daughter was living in. It was Shimshon who kept the peace but it was also Shimshon who had brought the unease. The Philistines couldn't bring advanced culture and civilisation to the whole area because the Hebrews wanted to keep their own culture and religious beliefs. And the Hebrews were able to hold the Philistine army at bay because they had Shimshon, the superman.

Abanata thought the whole situation was a mess, but one man couldn't live for ever and he hoped that his daughter would live most of her life in a Shimshon-free world. He took another look at D'lila, smiled and then went back to the vines. They wouldn't keep themselves tended, and these days he felt so tired; his body was riddled with aches and pains.

★ ★ ★

'She's the daughter of Abanata, the old vineyard grower from Sorek. She's a Philistine, mind you, so she won't be too pleased from any advance from you.'

It all felt like this had happened before, but those events seemed like another lifetime away for Shimshon. The past 20 years had gone by without any major incident. Since he had removed the gates from Gaza, the Philistines had lacked the courage to mount any major campaign against his people. Shimshon got the impression that they were waiting – waiting for the time when he was gone. Then they could move on God's land again.

And Shimshon was still alone. He still hadn't found a wife and now he was much older. He was still strong and still brought fear into the Philistines, but he had no wife and no children. He hadn't been blessed in that way.

So when the young woman had caught his eye, he thought maybe, just maybe, his time had come.

She had caught his eye in a similar way to the way Ba'alshada had and she was in the town to do some trading, although it wasn't her father she was with. At first he thought it might have been her husband, but by the way she was ordering the man around, he thought, or at least hoped, it was a servant.

But Shimshon wasn't the same naive young man he had been 20 years ago. This time he remembered to keep his mouth closed while he was drooling. He also managed to make it look like he wasn't staring at her. And finally, he chose a close and trusted Jewish trader to ask who the girl was.

'I tell you, her father won't want anything to do with you.' The trader's words stung Shimshon. Yet again he was falling for a woman not of his religion, but Shimshon hoped that history wouldn't repeat itself. This time he wouldn't demand a wedding, he wouldn't push the relationship through getting parents and business deals arranged. He would take things slowly and control the situation. That way nothing would go wrong.

Shimshon looked over at the woman again and had to turn away quickly as she stared straight back. He didn't think she had seen him, so he could still control the situation.

But first, duty called. There was news of some bandits operating in the area and the militia wanted some advice on how to deal with them. 'Politics,' he shook his head and left the town.

★ ★ ★

D'lila was in town again. She was hoping to see the mighty Shimshon again. Since she had spotted him on her last visit and had noticed him looking at her, she had been unable to think about much else. She had become almost obsessed about him, his history and his power.

She had tried to make excuses to get into town but one thing or another had conspired to stop her. So this was the first time she had been able to get out, with a legitimate excuse. Her father had seemed preoccupied when she left but hadn't minded when she suggested the trip into town.

And now, here she was waiting and hoping. There wasn't much to do since the errand she was running had taken only a few minutes to sort out. She had found out by a roundabout method, so as not to draw too much attention, that Shimshon, his advisors and some of the Judean milita regularly came through the town every few days. A visit was now due, and so she waited.

The sun was high in the sky and the day was becoming hot and balmy. But she didn't mind. She would suffer the heat and unpleasantness for a chance to see Shimshon. Perhaps he might notice her again.

She made her way to the well and lifted some water from deep within. She drank a little, feeling its coolness radiate out from her stomach. As she sat and sipped, she felt nothing in the world could go wrong.

'Mistress D'lila, you must come home at once.' The servant had rushed up and stood agitated in front of her. 'It's your father; he has collapsed in the field. He was brought back to the house, but he has no breath. You must come now.'

D'lila dropped her cup on the floor and the water seeped away into the sand. She jumped up and began to head home. All thoughts of the mighty Shimshon were replaced by the fear of losing her father.

★ ★ ★

Once again D'lila found herself back in town. This was the first trading visit she had done as owner of the vineyard, the vineyard that had once been her father's. He had not breathed since he had collapsed in the vineyard a month before. He had been buried days later and now that the mourning period was over, D'lila had taken responsibility for her father's estate, as she was the only child.

She also hoped that she may see Shimshon. Despite the despair she had felt recently, she had held onto seeing the Hebrew again and now that the time of mourning was over, she hoped she could continue her life. And perhaps Shimshon could be a part of that.

'I am sorry to hear about your loss.' The voice was deep and brought her out of the daydream she had slipped into. She jumped and then turned around to face the speaker. She looked right into the chest of a man, before raising her eyes to see that the chest belonged to Shimshon. She couldn't say anything.

'I am sorry for startling you.' The tall, muscular leader of the Jewish people looked sheepish as he spoke to her. 'I didn't mean to make you jump or scare you. But you seemed so far away in your thoughts that I was unsure how to approach you. In the end I just spoke. I have a habit of just doing what feels best. Once again, I am sorry.' Shimshon began to turn away and D'lila knew she had to say something if she was to keep him there.

'You're not as big in real life as the stories about you suggest.' As the words left her mouth she couldn't believe she had said them. 'I'm sorry... I meant that the stories about you make you out to be this amazing and great person.' She felt herself digging a hole and getting deeper and deeper. She was glad when his expression turned from the deep concern he had first shown to a simple grin.

'It's okay, I know what you mean. The stories always exaggerate,' and then for good measure he added, 'a little anyway.'

The joke broke the tension for D'lila and she was able to compose herself, although she felt like all her dreams had come true in one sweet moment. She giggled and wondered whether the word 'sweet' had ever been used around Shimshon before.

D'lila composed herself. 'Thank you for your concern. I have mourned my father's passing and now I have to look after the vineyard and support the household.' She stood straight but still didn't come any higher than Shimshon's shoulders. 'But there is a lot of work to do; looking after a farm isn't easy work.'

'I know, my parents had a farm and I helped on it for years until I…' Shimshon didn't continue the sentence and D'lila knew he was trying to be sensitive.

'Yes, I have heard the stories about your younger days. The one about you bringing your father's grain to trade on your back instead of in a cart was particularly amazing.'

'You shouldn't believe everything you hear. If I remember rightly, those journeys involved me, grain and a loveable old donkey that pulled the cart.' His smile made D'lila blush. He was certainly all that she had imagined him to be these past few weeks.

'If you'd accept my offer, I'd be willing to help in any way I can.'

D'lila tried not to leap with joy at Shimshon's kindness. After all, she didn't want to appear too eager to have the Hebrew in her presence. 'That would be perfectly acceptable.' She tried to look as coy as she could. 'Why don't you come and visit tomorrow? I'll have the servants prepare a meal and you can dispense your farming advice.'

She turned away from Shimshon with a huge smile on her face and she was sure that the warm feeling on her back was due to the smile on Shimshon's face.

The bales of wheat had proved an ideal hiding place. They were close enough to hear everything that the Philistine woman and Shimshon had said. And now, as they both left, Akron was able to relax and reflect on what he had heard.

Akron had been following Shimshon for years. His job was to find out what the Hebrew was doing and report back to Ba'alsherath, the Seranim of Ekron, the oldest and wisest of the five Seranims who were kings of the Philistine cities.

This could be just what they had been looking for. They knew that Shimshon had been involved with a Philistine woman before. In fact, that had started Shimshon's reign of terror.

Akron hadn't had anything significant to report back before, but now, that had changed. He got up from his concealed position and began to plan his journey back to Ekron, and thought of how he might spend his reward.

The plot

Abad shifted his weight on the cushions, trying to get more comfortable. Where is the cup-bearer? he thought. He waved his arm impatiently and a servant came rushing up with a jug. The wine didn't taste as sweet as normal and the fish course he had eaten had left him with indigestion.

Abad belched, which drew sycophantic laughter from the other four city state rulers. Abad ruled Gaza, and, currently, he was still the wealthiest and therefore the most powerful person in the room. But that wealth was diminishing. Abad's father had been the Seranim when the superman Shimshon had led the Hebrews to revolt and stop paying tribute. That was almost 20 years ago now and Abad was seeing power melt away.

He was nowhere near ruin. There was still plenty in the treasure vaults, but like his wine goblet, they would be emptied all too soon. And if Abad was concerned, the others seated around him would soon be mortified. He let his gaze roll over them one at a time. Ethlan of Askelon: like Abad, a young leader more prone to partying than leading. Alagon from Ashdod: a weasle of a man who Abad disliked only slightly less than the Hebrews. P'ternath of Gath: a short, tiny and calculating Seranim who Abad was sure wanted to find a way to make Gath the primary city state of Philistine. Abad almost laughed again as his eyes lingered on P'ternath – he was so short and weedy and yet the irony was, that so many of the men from Gath were tall and strong. Gath supplied the strongest warriors from all of Philistine, another reason to be wary of P'ternath.

Finally, there was Ba'alsherath, the oldest member of the group here, and the one who sucked up to Abad the least. Ba'alsherath had been leader for over 60 years. He had come to power while still a child and had been tutored in his role as he grew older. If money wasn't the overriding factor of hierarchy, Ba'alsherath would have been the patriarch of this little clan. In fact, as Abad looked at him now, he realised that Ba'alsherath was the leader. Quietly and with the least amount of fuss, he manipulated the rest of them to do his bidding.

Abad would have been concerned if it wasn't for the old man's age. He would be gone soon and Dagon had not blessed him with offspring. Abad would then use his wealth and influence to place a puppet in charge of Ekron, and then Abad would effectively rule the whole five city states – that is, if he could muscle in on P'ternath's rule.

Abad shook his jowly face. What was he thinking? He was getting ahead of himself. There was a more pressing problem than the future plans for the domination of

Philistia – Shimshon, the legend, the killer of Philistines and the saviour of the Hebrews. Abad saw the weakness in the Hebrews. They were fine when things were going well; when they had a leader, they'd worship their god. But they also got complacent. They would forget that they needed to remain vigilant, to look after their land and to thank their God. And Shimshon would be the same.

'Shimshon has fallen right into our hands,' declared Abad. Ethlon and Alagon cheered as the wine encouraged unconfirmed celebrations. P'terath raised his eyebrows and Ba'alsherath cocked his head to one side, considering Abad's words. 'The fool has let his hormones take control once again. Word has reached me that he has fallen for a woman from the Valley of Sorok.' Ethlon and Alagon continued their joviality. How Abad would love to wipe the smile off Alagon's face, but that would have to wait.

'In what way does that help us?'

Abad knew that P'terath would raise a question, so he was unfazed by the Seranim's words. 'My dear brother,' Abad said ingratiatingly, enjoying the fact that he had one up on Gath's shortest, 'Shimshon will come closer to us than he has for ages. The Valley of Sorok is within striking distance from here. A small contingent of our best warriors can catch Shimshon unawares, kill him and then we can strike back at the Hebrews.'

P'ternath wanted to argue but the plan did have legs, and as long as he didn't have to do any fighting that was good too. He pondered who, out of his elite guard, he could send to do the job and rid the Philistines of this infernal menace. Abad's words broke his concentration, 'Once again Philistia will make the Hebrews pay tribute and work for them; once again we will prove our greatness.' Four of the Seranims raised their goblets and downed the wine. One hesitated.

'Your plan has merit and could work,' Ba'alsherath quietly interjected. Before Abad could be offended at any slight to his plan, Ba'alsherath continued. 'My concern is that Shimshon has proved time and again his great strength. What if the forces we send are again thwarted by his power? I know he is older now than the last time he slaughtered our men, but we should be cautious.' Abad put his goblet down and cleared his throat to respond. But Ba'alsherath held up a wrinkled hand. 'Please, Abad, I have every faith in our men and your leadership.' Abad was sure he heard P'ternath sniff at that, but he let Ba'alsherath continue.

'Listen to an old man, one who has seen many fights, but one who has the grey hair that only wisdom brings.' Abad thought the old man was more white-haired than grey, but he let him continue. 'I haven't survived all these years through rushing into fights. Victory is often given to the one who has god on his side.'

At this Abad jumped in, 'Then victory is ours for sure. Shimshon is a heathen since he worships the invisible Hebrew God. Dagon has been proved mighty by giving us this land and providing our needs. He protected our ancestors as they journeyed across the sea and gave them this land, Philistia. Time and time again, he has delivered the Hebrews into our hands and he will deliver them again.' Abad shocked himself at the level of faith he was showing. His old priest-tutor would be proud.

Ba'alaherath nodded, but as he raised his hand again, one finger outstretched and tapping the air, he wasn't in full agreement. 'Again you are correct in what you say. Dagon and the other gods in their heavenly realm have been good to us; they have also judged us harshly when we have rushed ahead without their blessing.' Ba'alasherath exhaled deeply. Abad was surprised that the old man's frail frame didn't rattle; he was obviously stronger than he looked.

'Shimshon may not have faith in one of our gods, but I have heard he does have faith, and I tend to believe this rather than the stories about him being over ten feet tall and even broader still.' Ba'alahserath repeated himself, 'I have heard that Shimshon believes his strength comes from his God. However ridiculous that sounds to us, he believes it. He believes his strength is a gift.' The old

Seranim paused for effect, letting the information sink into the other city lords.

'If we could find out the secret of his strength and somehow destroy that faith, then there would be no need to risk another confidence-destroying defeat at that animal's hands.' The acid was clear in Ba'alsherath's voice. Abad realised why the old man was still lord of Ekron. He looked old, frail and as if the slightest wind would do irreparable damage, but his heart and mind were as strong as ever.

Abad seemed at once, sober; the effect of the wine suddenly forgotten. He shifted forward on his cushions, a grin growing on his face. Across from the food spread before them, Ba'asherath met Abad's grin with one of his own. The old man's eyes were alive. 'The girl is the key, if we can get her to help us...' Ba'alasherath stopped talking, encouraging the grinning Seranim opposite him to take control of the planning again. He was aware that Abad could be a good and powerful leader of the city states and he didn't want to jeopardise that by taking all the glory for Shimshon's defeat.

Abad took up the challenge, 'Yes, the girl. I have heard, although this may be hearsay, that she has been resisting Shimshon's advances. Perhaps the affection is more one-sided than the Hebrew would like to think.' Abad's mind spun with the possibilities. If she wasn't totally committed to Shimshon, then a little persuasion would gain her assistance and if there was one thing Abad knew, it was how to persuade people.

'My fellow Seranim, this is a great day – today we plan to take back the tribute paid by the Hebrews.' All four of the Seranims looked at him expectantly. 'Gentlemen, if you could give me a little money, then I think we'll be on the way to ridding ourselves of Shimshon.'

* * *

Shennahgon straightened his iron mail tunic, made sure his sword scabbard was pushed firmly to the side and removed his feathered helmet. He was still sweating and breathing heavily from the horse ride back to Gaza. But when the Seranim demanded your immediate presence, you came without a thought for personal hygiene and fashion. He hoped that he didn't look too dishevelled and dishonour his lord.

'I have been called by the Seranim.' The servant bowed and turned. He entered the hall beyond, slipping through the thick purple curtains like a snake. The guards either side of the opening stood passively. They had nothing to fear with Shennahgon; after all, he was their commander.

The Captain of the Guard turned and paced in front of the soldiers, his helmet tucked under his arm. He tried to calm his breathing, using all his military training skills to quieten his mind and body for what lay ahead.

The servant returned, again slinking through the curtains without parting them. He nodded to Shennahgon and without a word pulled one of the curtains to one side. Silently, Shennahgon approached the opening and stepped through.

The hall beyond wasn't just large, it was cavernous. Shennahgon had been here before, several times for official functions, but never for this, a one-to-one with the Seranim. On his previous visits the hall had been full of dignitaries, sycophants and minions. He had been one of many. Because of this, the hall hadn't seemed so large. Now even his breathing seemed to echo in the space. His leather footfalls pounded on the stone floor and the sound reverberated around.

Ahead of him stood several of the Seranim's court – they were huddled to one side of a raised dais. They were discussing something but, even in this echoing cavern, their voices were so hushed, they made little noise.

At the centre of the dais was the throne. Seranim Abad, lord of Gaza, and would-be ruler of the Philistine people, sat upon it. Shennahgon sensed all this with his peripheral vision, for no one looked directly at the Seranim.

'Captain, I thank you for coming so quickly.' The Seranim's voice echoed in the hall. 'We have an opportunity to move against Shimshon. We have found out that he has become friendly with a Philistine woman and we want you to get her to help us. If she can find out the secret of his strength, then we can trap him and make him our prisoner. The Hebrews will no longer have a leader. They will fall apart and once again the Philistine nation can rule.'

Shennahgon's spirit rose. For 20 years he had waited to avenge his father's death, so any opportunity or chance to take that was uplifting.

'My servants have a casket of gold and silver for you to take and use to encourage the woman to help us. I am sure you know how important this is to Philistia. But also think about yourself, too. I want this to work and when it does, the rewards will not be limited to the woman. I hope you understand what I mean.'

Shennahgon nodded while still bowing. It wasn't his right to respond verbally to Abad.

'Good. Now go and find out the secret of Shimshon. And when you do, bring him to me and we'll sacrifice him to our gods.'

Shennahgon backed out of the hall, finding it difficult to contain the excitement of finally getting the chance to destroy Shimshon, just as the Hebrew had destroyed his father.

★ ★ ★

Shennahgon had his orders, but he wanted to know if this was the time. Was almost 20 years waiting for revenge about to come to an end? So, just like his father did 20 years before, he went to the temple to ask the gods what the future had in store.

Just like his father, he made the offering to Dagon and the priest prepared the chicken for the ritual. As the entrails were laid out on the stone and the priest threw the dust into the flaming bowl, Shennahgon waited for the future to be revealed.

The priest prodded and pulled at the grizzly mess on the stone while muttering the words designed to placate the spirits.

'The future is becoming clearer.' The priest dropped some more dust into the flame to produce another bright display of coloured smoke. 'The gods are with you and they favour you. Your mission will be a success.' The priest raised his eyes to look directly at the soldier. 'Revenge will be yours; Dagon goes with you.'

Shennahgon thanked the priest and left the temple. He had waited for Dagon to show him the time was right, and now, after 20 years, it was. Now it was time to make Shimshon pay for killing his father.

★ ★ ★

The Captain of the Guard had arrived unannounced and under the semi-cover of twilight. He now stood in front of D'lila. It was a few days since Shimshon had last visited D'lila and the Hebrew was due to return soon. They had got on reasonably well and D'lila thought they could have a future together, although Shimshon's religious beliefs had worried her. He seemed to completely ignore the beliefs of her people. Perhaps two cultures couldn't exist too closely.

D'lila knew that the Captain's visit was to do with her interest in Shimshon, but she didn't know exactly what he wanted from her. And the way Shannahgon spoke she wouldn't find out too soon. The Captain had a long speech that was designed to bring her around to his way of thinking.

She listened to what he was saying while sipping some of the wine from her own vineyard. That was another thing about Shimshon, she mused – he didn't touch wine. How could they ever be happy together if he'd never touch the produce of her land? She was fast slipping out of her crush on the Hebrew.

Shennahgon continued his speech but the words began to blur for D'lila. She caught snatches as his voice droned on.

'It is time for Philistia to rise again, the priests of Dagon have foreseen… The Hebrews are unorganised, a tribal race with no overall leadership. They have no king and no aspirations for a king... Remember how good things were under the rule of Philistia. Times were good, people prospered, your family prospered, you prospered ... Under Abad's leadership, Philistia could become a great nation, and people will once again prosper and be wealthy... Think of what a young lady like yourself could do in such a prosperous climate, especially if she found herself with a little wealth to start with?'

D'lila's concentration returned. Shennahgon had put a casket down before her and opened it, before once again standing. The light from the oil lamps flickered on the contents of the casket and the light rebounded around the room.

'And what would you want me to do?'

'We know that there is a reason for Shimshon's strength. We have heard rumours from our contacts in the Judean militia that Shimshon has a secret and that is why he is so strong. He isn't any bigger than some of our soldiers in Gath and yet his strength is immense. Your job is to get him to trust you and then find out his secret.'

D'lila looked at the open casket. Inside, the gold and silver shimmered like waves in the shallows. She noticed that her tongue had slipped onto her bottom lip and was licking across her mouth, so she immediately bit down on the lower lip and turned around. D'lila suspected that the Captain had seen her response; she had looked far too keen. If she was to deceive Shimshon she would need to be a lot cleverer than that.

'I'll give you some of my most trusted men to help you. They can pretend to be hired helpers on the vineyard. But when you find out the secret of Shimshon's strength they can capture him for us.'

D'lila didn't want to hurt Shimshon, but she realised that she would be one of the wealthiest women around if things worked out well.

'Are you going to kill Shimshon?' She asked the question to Shennahgon's face and looked deep into his eyes as he prepared to answer.

'I promise you that Shimshon will not be killed here. We will take him to Seranim Abad. The city lord wants to see him. I believe that without his power, Shimshon will become nothing and there will be no need to kill him.'

D'lila could see no element of deception in the Captain's eyes. But then 20 years of waiting for the right moment to seek his revenge had left Shennahgon cold and calculating. No one could see anything in his eyes.

'Send your men. I'll find out Shimshon's secret.'

Teased

D'lila's house was large with many rooms. There were also several houses where other servants and vineyard workers lived. After his initial visit, Shimshon had gone back to the Judean militia and told them that he was taking a break for a while. There was some family business he needed to sort out. He would return soon, but for a while they would need to look after themselves.

Now he was here. He was able to devote his time to D'lila and convince her to be with him, to become his wife and to find faith in the true and only God, Adonai.

He had offered his knowledge and skill as a farmer to obtain the invite back to D'lila's home, but it seemed she was in little need of help. Her vineyard had plenty of strong helpers and everything seemed to be running smoothly. All this added to Shimshon's peace of mind about everything. She had invited him back, but she didn't need his help, so she was obviously interested in him as a person.

They had spent the evening enjoying the food that D'lila's servants had prepared. Shimshon was sure that the evening had gone well. D'lila had spent a lot of time asking about Adonai and the history of his people. She was very interested in their beliefs and customs, especially about Shimshon's own spirituality as a Nazirite.

Now they sat together and tiredness was beginning to creep up on him.

'I heard that you were tied up and bound by the Judean militia when you met the Philistine army in the valley. And yet you managed to break free. Tell me the secret of your great strength. How were they not able to tie you up and keep you tied up?

Shimshon's head was drifting in and out of sleep. He opened his eyes and smiled at her.

'The way to tie me up and make me as weak as any other man is to use seven new bowstrings that haven't yet been dried. You want to tie me up and keep me tied, then that is the way.'

'Oh you are so silly,' D'lila said and kissed him on the forehead. Shimshon slowly fell into a deep sleep, his contentment shown by the grin on his face.

The Hebrew had fallen asleep and from the grin on his face, D'lila thought he was having some pleasant dream. She slipped out of her house to talk to one of the guards Shennahgon had sent to help her.

'I need seven new bowstrings that haven't been dried out. That's how we can capture Shimshon.'

The guard went back to his own outhouse and returned after a few minutes with the strings. 'I don't see how these are going to hold the Hebrew though; they aren't any stronger than other pieces of rope.'

'I don't know either, but the Hebrew trusts me and this is what he said. I'll tie him up and then, when I know his strength has gone I'll call you in – you wait outside the main room.'

D'lila returned to the room and began to wrap the bowstrings around Shimshon. She was able to pass the strings beneath him to hold his shoulders and around his wrists. The Hebrew was tied up.

D'lila stood back and then shouted, 'Shimshon, quick! Help! It's the Philistines; they are upon you!'

Shimshon woke with a start, leapt up and the strings fell apart as if they were strands of dry grass. He looked around the room, but there was only D'lila there. She looked at him and then at the bowstrings on the ground.

'You lied to me. How could you do that?' D'lila cried and stormed from the room to her own bedroom, leaving Shimshon half-awake and confused.

★ ★ ★

Breakfast had been brought in by the servants and there was an uneasy silence between Shimshon and D'lila. She was picking at her food and eating very little.

Shimshon found this hard to take as he was ravenous and was eating like he hadn't had a meal in days.

'What's wrong?' he asked after her umpteenth sigh of the morning. It seemed like she had been storing up her response and, like a burst dam, her words now poured out.

'You have made a fool out of me. Worse than that, you lied to me!'

The force of her outburst took Shimshon by surprise and he was unable to respond for a few moments.

'You mean last night? How was I to know that you were going to tie me up and test what I had said? If anyone should be upset it is me. I was the one being tied up.' His words led to an uneasy truce for the rest of the morning, but by midday, she was again asking how he could be tied up. He was beginning to get tired of the question.

'I need to be tied securely with ropes that have never been used. If that is done then I'll become as weak as any other man,' snapped Shimshon.

D'lila said nothing more about the ropes for the rest of the day and by the evening the atmosphere had relaxed again. They spent a nice evening once again talking about life, the world and everything. Shimshon fell asleep, content once more that all was right and things were going to work out well between him and D'lila.

Once again D'lila went to the soldiers and got some unused rope. Shimshon slept so soundly that tying him up was easy. She stepped back from him and shouted the same warning as the night before.

Shimshon leapt from his slumber and yet again snapped the ropes like they were thin sewing threads. D'lila ran from the room, her face in her hands, mock tears flowing from her eyes. She hoped the act was playing on Shimshon.

* * *

After the previous day, when D'lila had sulked to get her own way, she decided to be straight and obvious.

'Did you sleep well last night? No restrictions I hope.' She handed Shimshon some bread to eat for his breakfast and gave him a big smile. The visible and audible sigh was exactly what she hoped for. She had wanted Shimshon to see that she wasn't overly disappointed, but that she was playing a game with him. She wanted him relaxed about the whole situation and didn't want him to become suspicious as to her real reason for finding his secret.

At lunchtime, they had gone into the town to buy some supplies from the traders. D'lila made a point of flattering and flirting with Shimshon as they journeyed together. And after they had got the supplies and were heading back, she made her move.

'You are such a tease you know,' she tapped his chin playfully with her finger.

'What do you mean?' Shimshon adjusted the sack that he had offered to carry on his shoulders, as if to make out it was actually heavy.

'Just that. That sack isn't heavy for you. Your strength is greater than anyone I know, and if I understand rightly you'd like to use that strength to look after me and my vineyard.' D'lila paused letting the words register with Shimshon. She hoped he would take the bait and see how serious she was about their relationship. 'But you keep making a fool out of me. Saying that new bowstrings or unused rope can keep you tied up. Rope isn't the secret to your strength and you know it. You've been lying to me. Why won't you tell me how you can be tied?'

Shimshon laughed and looked at her. 'It isn't about being tied at all, is it?'

D'lila almost stopped in shock as she thought that Shimshon was on to her.

'It's about my strength, isn't it? You want to know the secret of my strength.' A cute smile flashed across his face and he shook his head. The braids whipped through the air. 'It's all in my hair.' Shimshon bit his lip and then added, 'If you weave the seven braids of my hair into the fabric on a loom and then tighten it with a pin, I'll be as weak as any other man.'

When they got back to the vineyard, Shimshon helped dig a new irrigation trench, while D'lila got everything ready for the evening and night. After a tiring afternoon and a veritable feast of an evening meal, Shimshon once again fell asleep.

D'lila took some time in weaving his braids on the small loom and then tightening it all up with a pin. When she had finished she thought Shimshon looked stupid with the material in his hair, but not any weaker.

'Shimshon, the Philistines are upon you!'

The loom went flying across the room as Shimshon rose up, no weaker than he had ever been. He laughed at D'lila and the expression she gave him. So she stormed from the room, slamming the wooden door as she left.

★ ★ ★

Day after day, D'lila asked Shimshon where his strength came from and day after day he refused to tell her. But the relentless questioning began to take its toll. Shimshon had to make a decision or all of this would drive him mad. But what should he do? Tell her the truth? At least that would stop all this nagging…

'I was thinking about what you said on the journey home the other day, about me looking after you. And…' Shimshon found it hard to say it, but he knew he had to, 'I do want to be with you. I love you, D'lila.'

D'lila bit her lip and seemed to be thinking. Shimshon hoped she would forgive him about the loom incident and admit that she loved him too and wanted to be with him.

'How can you say that you love me when you won't even confide in me about the truth? Again you have made a fool out of me and not told me the secret of your strength.'

'OK, OK.' Shimshon had had enough. If he had to tell her the truth to stop her from asking him, and to admit that she loved him, then so be it.

'It is my hair – that much was true. No razor has ever been used on my head. It's all part of the Nazirite vow that set me apart from birth. If my head were shaved, my strength would leave me. With no hair, I would be as weak as any other man.'

It worked.

'Oh Shimshon, I'm sorry to have kept going on, but we should be open with each other. A couple should never keep secrets. I love you, too.'

Shimshon relaxed and looked forward to a wonderful future with D'lila. Perhaps the Philistines weren't all bad; perhaps there was a future between the two peoples.

Forsaken

D'lila sent Shimshon out to find a goat from the far field so they could celebrate with a large meal. While he was gone, she called one of the soldiers Shennahgon had left with her. She told him to go and get Shennahgon and the silver; she had found out the secret of Shimshon's strength.

★ ★ ★

That evening, after the dinner, D'lila and Shimshon went for a walk in the cooling air. The meal had been excessive and D'lila had seen that Shimshon was celebrating the breakthrough in their relationship. As they walked, D'lila kept seeing things that needed picking up or moving and asked Shimshon, 'her strong man', to do the honours. She wanted him as tired as possible when he finally fell asleep.

They spent the later part of the evening talking and once again Shimshon fell into a sleep, this time helped by D'lila holding him and letting him rest his weary head in her lap.

When the Hebrew began to snore, Shennahgon and the soldiers entered the room on cue. D'lila called Shennahgon over with a flick of her head.

'It's his hair,' she whispered. 'If we shave off his hair, he'll be as weak as anyone else.'

Shennahgon looked shocked for a moment and then got one of the men to cut off the long braids. When that was done they began to gently tie him with some strong rope. Everyone was still extremely nervous about Shimshon. He could wake at any moment and they could find out that another lie had been told. When Shimshon was bound, the man who had cut the braids used an extremely sharp knife to shave his hair even shorter; they wanted to make no mistakes.

Finally, Shimshon lay in D'lila's lap, still asleep and still snoring but with very little hair on his head. He looked like a helpless baby, albeit over 40 years old and rippling with muscles.

The soldiers Shennahgon had brought were some of the biggest and strongest soldiers he could find, a few of them from Gath where big soldiers seemed to fall out of the woodwork. Now they all stood around the sleeping giant. They were about to find out if what Shimshon had told D'lila was true.

The muddiness and murkiness of being asleep to the crispness and clearness of being awake took only moments. But for Shimshon, it seemed like an eternity. It began with his name being called, pulling him from a dream he had been having about foxes who could talk, complaining about being mistreated.

For a brief time he thought it was the foxes calling, before losing the thread of his dream and swimming into consciousness.

'Shimshon!' He thought he recognised the voice; yes, it was someone he knew. Then it flooded into his mind. Not just someone he knew but someone he loved. It was D'lila. But why was she calling him? What did she want?

'Shimshon, it's the Philistines; they are here and they are upon you.'

Shimshon awoke. However, something was strange; he still felt tired. He thought nothing of it and began to smile – she was testing him again. She still hadn't believed what he had told her. Of course, that was understandable, considering the lies he had fed her this past week or so.

As he smiled, he tried to push himself up from lying down, but he couldn't move his arms. He squeezed his eyes shut to rid them of the final vestiges of sleep and then opened them wide.

His eyes opened and at the same time he felt himself lifted up from D'lila's lap. He looked straight into the eyes of a Philistine soldier. The soldier had lifted him up by using the rope that was tied around Shimshon. Shimshon flexed his muscles, but the rope wouldn't break. In fact, it would hardly flex or bend. Shimshon was tied up and couldn't break free.

The first blow took him by surprise. He had never felt real pain before; he had always been the one inflicting it. More punches and kicks landed on his body and the pain seared through his body. He could feel his skin splitting as pressure pounded onto it with punch after punch.

Darkness began to grab Shimshon once more, but it wasn't sleep that was beckoning, it was unconsciousness. Shimshon had lost his strength and he was no stronger than anyone else. As the pain increased, Shimshon cried out, 'Adonai, why have you deserted me?'

And with that, he passed out.

★ ★ ★

Had it been moments, minutes or hours? Shimshon didn't know. But as the world swam slowly back into existence around him, he knew that he was in trouble. He also knew that he had been unconscious, so why was he upright and moving? As clarity crystallised, the answer revealed itself.

He was moving but his feet weren't the reason. They hung limply beneath his body. He knew this because he was looking straight at them. Shimshon glanced to his left and saw sandaled feet pacing next to his dragged pair. He switched his view to the right and saw an almost duplicate image, although these feet were attached to slightly hairier legs. Hair.

Shimshon tried to raise his head, but it refused, like a door still held by its wooden barrier. Instead, he used his eyes that seemed to obey his commands to see more. His own body looked battered and bruised. A long gash down his right thigh was marked by congealed blood that looked like red honey. There were several smaller cuts as his eyes surveyed his frame.

He noticed his hands flush with the top of his thighs, unnaturally close, as if they were... his mind couldn't focus. Like his legs, his hands looked like they'd been in a battle; they too were covered in cuts and scratches. They also seemed unnaturally dark. Shimshon wasn't fair by any standards, but the hands looked darker than usual. As he focused he realised they were numb too, dark and numb. It was as if the circulation wasn't working properly, the blood and ability to control his hands being thwarted by something. It was as if they were... tied.

The ropes began just above his wrists. They were cutting into his flesh and holding his hands, and arms, tight against his body. As he raised his eyes he noticed that the ropes continued right up his body as far as he could see. He couldn't see above his chest without moving his head. Shimshon put all his effort into getting movement back. Pain flared in his neck as the muscles strained. His vision dimmed with the effort, but slowly his head began to raise.

As his vision cleared, he squeezed his eyes shut to rid them of the last vestige of unconsciousness. He opened them and began to see where he was going. Shimshon was heading down a corridor. He was inside a building somewhere, but he didn't recognise it. His view bobbed up and down, and the vision was making him feel nauseous. He then remembered he wasn't walking.

Shimshon put all his effort into moving his head. Again the darkness threatened to take him under its control, but he fought it and as his head moved, he came face to face with a Philistine soldier. Despite having next to no control over his body, Shimshon managed to tense and pull away. The soldier simply tightened his grip on Shimshon's arm. Shaking the ropes that he held and which bound Shimshon, the soldier reaffirmed who was in control here. Shimshon was fast recovering. He turned his head to the right and saw another Philistine soldier holding his other arm. This one, the hairy one, was tall and broad just like his accomplice – probably from Gath, thought Shimshon.

They were dragging Shimshon, one on each arm. 'Seeing as you're awake,' Hairy said, 'you can do some of the work and let my arms have a rest.' The two soldiers came to a halt and let go. Shimshon dropped like a lead weight testing the water's depth. His whole body cried out in pain. It seemed like every muscle and sinew was being stabbed with a blade. The pain once again threatened to pull Shimshon into the darkness. He didn't believe he could feel more pain, but a fresh wave flared like wild fire in his side and he cried out.

Hairy's foot hit Shimshon just in front of his bound arm, catching him below the ribs.

'Get up.'

The words were spat at Shimshon but their force had no effect.

'I said get up.'

Both Hairy and the other soldier reached down and pulled Shimshon from the floor. They held him as they had been when he was being dragged. This time, though, they manoeuvred him like a rag doll, lifting him off the ground and then lowering him onto his own feet. Shimshon's feet began to buckle beneath him, but the soldiers took the slack.

'I'll say this just once,' Shimshon could feel Hairy's words on the side of his face. He could also smell the Philistine's last meal as Hairy's breath floated across Shimshon's face. 'My arms are getting tired. Now it's your turn to walk.'

Judging by the ease with which the two soldiers had lifted Shimshon from the floor, he doubted the authenticity of Hairy's claim, but the pain within

Shimshon's body meant that he was in no fit state to argue. Gritting his teeth and preparing his mind to hear the cry of pain from his body, Shimshon began to put some weight on his legs. His eyes closed as the pain flared upward from his feet, multiplied through his upper legs and reached a crescendo through his spine. Shimshon's cry was dry and hoarse and echoed down the corridor.

'There, that wasn't too bad, was it?' Hairy laughed and the other soldier joined in with a sound that showed he was probably more interested in disembowelling techniques than the discussion of philosophical issues. The two soldiers began their journey again, forcing their captive to join in. Shimshon took one painful step after another. His body cried out each time his legs were made to lift and then plant a foot.

As they made their way along the corridor Shimshon's head lolled to one side and then the other. On top of the pain and disorientation that he felt, Shimshon had a nagging thought that began to surface. There was another problem, but he couldn't quite figure it out. Sense was now flooding back in waves. Somehow they had managed to capture him and bind him, but how... the memory was a haze. He searched the fog but the images weren't clear. His head lolled to the side again; there was something missing; his head felt strange. What was wrong?

'No!'

Shimshon's cry bounced off the corridor walls. It all came back to him. His head lolled back the other side and once again the strange feeling was felt – the strange feeling that was caused by not feeling his braided hair move on his head. That feeling had been with him since birth and now it was gone. That feeling was what confirmed his allegiance with his God; that feeling was a sign of his strength; and that feeling, just like his hair and just like his strength and therefore just like his God, was gone. Could things get any worse?

★ ★ ★

The soldiers led Shimshon down the corridor, which was sparsely lit by torches every hundred cubits or so. They came to a heavy wooden door which Shimshon knew was a prison cell. Normally that door would hold no fear for the Hebrew, but now, without his strength, he was as vulnerable as anyone.

The door was unbolted; they had obviously been expecting Shimshon. There was even less light in here than in the corridor, but his eyes adjusted quickly to take in his new surroundings. Hairy and his companion kept a firm hold on their prisoner and turned him back toward the door they had just come through. As Shimshon faced the door he realised that they had been followed down the corridor by several others. The first of these now entered.

Shennahgon stepped through the door and removed his helmet. Shimshon blinked his eyes in the dim light and took in the features of the Captain of the Guard. He recognised him, but from where? His mind was still a mess, but the memory slowly formed. He had seen this man at D'lila's; he was there when he had woken up. This man had led the force of soldiers that had captured him and beaten him, and obviously brought him here, wherever here was.

'Welcome to Gath, Shimshon.' Well that answered one of the questions Shimshon had. 'Or more precisely, the dungeons in the Seranim's palace. I hope the journey from Sorek wasn't too uncomfortable. An overnight journey pulled in a wagon behind some horses isn't the most glamorous way to travel.' The Captain moved closer to Shimshon, his face inches away, 'Do you recognise me from last night?' Shimshon nodded slightly. 'But I don't suppose you recognise me from before then?' Shimshon searched his memory but came up blank; he wasn't that big on remembering the faces of Philistine soldiers.

'We've met before, albeit indirectly and at a distance.' The revelation didn't help Shimshon place the Captain. 'About 20 years ago, when you overturned the tribute deal of your people, there was a fight.' Shimshon remembered the fight well enough, but he still couldn't recognise the soldier. By the looks of the soldier he would have been barely out of his teens at that time. 'About 20 years ago you killed a lot of people.' The captain was right in front of Shimshon now, his breath raising goose bumps on Shimshon's skin.

'Let me tell you a little more. On that day, in that fight, there was another Captain of the Guard involved. A man named Addad'agon.' Shimshon remembered the previous Captain; he could see his face. As he recalled the Captain he began to see a resemblance, a similar small nose, the same deep set eyes, even the tone of skin, despite the dark. 'Is it coming back now?' Shennahgon continued without waiting for an answer, 'That was my father.'

Outside the cell, Shimshon heard some noise. Something was going on, but he needed to deflect the Captain's anger. There was something sinister in the way he was speaking. For the first time in his life, Shimshon felt frightened.

'My God wanted his people to be free. We are meant to pay tribute and give praise to God, not other people. Your people, including your father, wouldn't let that happen. You made the choice,' he said.

Shennahgon's expression hadn't changed and he gave no impression that he had listened to or heard anything that Shimshon had said. 'And you made the choice to serve your god.' The Captain's words surprised Shimshon, 'and that, my friend, was your mistake.' Shennahgon stared deep into Shimshon's face. The stare was cold; the only thing it conveyed was menace. 'Oh yes, that was your mistake, because your god isn't here now.'

Shennahgon turned and headed for the cell door. Outside came the noise once again and as Shimshon looked past the Captain, he saw an eerie glow from the corridor. The Captain disappeared and all Shimshon could see were shadows flickering on the wall outside. Two more guards came into the cell and joined Hairy and his friend in holding Shimshon.

The Captain returned and Shimshon immediately began to struggle, 'My God, why have you left me?' The guards held him tighter as Shennahgon approached. In his hand was an iron fire poker, its end white-hot. 'Your god won't help you and now justice will be served.' Shennahgon raised the poker toward Shimshon's face. 'You took my father away from me and I'll never see him again.' The poker was now just in front of Shimshon, 'and now you'll never see again.'

Hairy and the other original guard held Shimshon's head back and forced his eyes open. Shennahgon pushed the poker toward the left eye of Shimshon. The light grew larger and brighter, the soldiers held Shimshon's head tight as it shook to try and move out of the way. As the iron plunged into Shimshon's eye, there was a moment of surprise as he felt the eyeball pop and its contents ooze down his cheek. Then the pain flared. It was so intense that he failed to realise the other eye had gone through a similar fate. There were two stages of darkness, the first as he lost his sight, the second as he passed out with the pain and fell to the floor of the cell. Shennahgon and the guards left, the door was bolted and Shimshon lay on the floor, alone.

* * *

'Time to get up.' The voice was Hairy's. This was the nightmare that Shimshon could not wake up from. 'You're off to Gaza.' The ropes were still tight around Shimshon's body. He wanted to reply with one of his usual self-confident retorts, but the fight wasn't in him. His head throbbed and the pain echoed around the darkness that was now his daily existence.

He had been betrayed by the woman he loved and now he had let his people down. He knew that the Philistines would build another army and then begin to attack the Israelites once more. His only hope was that the Israelites were now more prepared to fight back; he had shown them how to be courageous once more, and worship their true God.

When he arrived at Gaza, he realised he was being led deep into the prison, for he could hear the other prisoners jeering him. They put shackles on his ankles and wrists. He was going nowhere now.

'Seranim Abad will want to see you, but he is busy resting at the moment. So while you're here you'll be doing the manual work. We need someone who has the strength of an ox to turn the grinding stones. Oh, I'm sorry; I forgot you don't have that strength anymore. Still at least you look like an ox – that'll do.'

Shimshon was set to work, chained and hopeless.

The sky will fall

It seemed like months had passed while Shimshon pushed the grinding stones, and it may have been. Time no longer held any meaning for Shimshon, nor did his life.

'C'mon you, you're going to see, oh I'm sorry, did I say see? I forgot you can't see. And even if you did have eyes, you don't look at the Seranim. Yes, that's right; you're going to the temple today. We're going to thank Dagon for all he has done for us, and that means giving us you.'

Shimshon's failure was complete. He had let himself down, he had let his people down, but most of all, he had let God down. With the strength God had given him, he should have been an unbeatable leader, but he had put himself first and because of his own needs he had forgotten the needs of others. And now look where he was – the irony brought only regret.

He was led like a dog from the prison and, he assumed, into the temple. His hearing was more acute now, compensating for his lack of sight, but he hadn't worked on using it to tell his surroundings. He could hear the jeering and cheering though, as he was led into a large hall or arena of some sort.

He knew that the temple of Dagon had a large central area. The roof was supported by two central pillars. The roof of the temple was also used by people when there was no room left in the terraces that surrounded the arena – it was part closed and part open. Those who had climbed up the outside of the temple could look down on the proceedings. At one end, above the main open entrance, the royal dignitaries sat. Shimshon had heard that an image of the sky had been painted on the closed area of the roof, but he knew he would never see that. His humiliation was complete.

He felt the breeze from the main entrance as it blew across the arena. It licked around his body lifting the hair on his legs, arms and chest. But it didn't lift the hair on his head.

Shimshon had been so engrossed in his own failure that he had missed the Philistine's failure. They had cut his hair at the house of the betrayer, but they hadn't cut it since. Shimshon began to wander around the temple, to the amusement of the Philistines.

'What's wrong, Shimshon? Is your God not guiding you any more?!'

'Oi, Shimshon! Looking for another Philistine woman to fall in love with?'

He sensed his way to the centre of the arena and the two pillars. 'Where are the pillars, I need to support myself.'

One of the temple prostitutes danced around him and heard his request. She began to push him in the direction of the pillars, her dance enticing the crowd to cheer all the more. She flitted around the helpless muscular man. 'Dagon be praised!' echoed around the temple. The crowds loved it and they laughed as the blind superman was directed by the temple dancers.

He made it to the pillars and he placed his hands on them.

'Oh Yahweh, my Adonai, please remember me.' Shimshon's prayer was said between sobs, the cry of someone truly sorry for what they had done. 'I have done wrong and I have neglected my promise and vow to you; please forgive me.' The sobs continued. 'Adonai, I ask you to give me strength one last time, to avenge them for what they have done to my eyes.'

For the first time in months, Shimshon felt a familiar tingle through his body as his muscles regained their strength. He braced himself between the pillars and thanked God for rescuing his people from the false rule and false god of the Philistines.

He raised his head to where he thought the Seranim and the other leaders were sitting. He imagined looking right at them. He began to smile and then let the smile turn to a grimace as he began to push against the pillars. He thought he heard one lone cry of concern from the royal enclosure, but he wasn't sure.

At first, the pillars resisted Shimshon's pressure, but then, amongst all the cheering and abuse levelled at Shimshon, he heard the first crack. Shimshon pushed harder.

'Yahweh is my God; I shall worship no other. This is the land you promised to our ancestors. The people of this land shall worship no other.' His voice rumbled and so did the temple.

The two pillars were moving under Shimshon's strength and bits of stone and mortar were beginning to fall around him.

The main support pillars held the whole roof onto the temple. The people on the roof couldn't see the pillars move, as the pillars were under part of the enclosed roof; however, they felt them. The roof lurched first one way, then the other, and then it began to fall.

A nursing mother had cheered as the Hebrew blundered his way across the arena, but her cheers turned to screams as the baby slipped from her arms. The baby screamed because it was no longer feeding and the mother screamed as she saw the infant fall to the floor. Within moments though, her screams were for herself as her own vantage point was upended and she dropped like a stone. Mother and baby were reunited in a crushed mess of flesh and fabric.

The prostitute who had led Shimshon to the pillars raised her hands in fright as she realised what was happening. The mild hallucinogenic drug which they used in the temple for their rituals didn't take away the fear; it exaggerated it. She backed away from Shimshon and thought about running away. A body landed next to her and her sheer dress was spattered with the blood as the body split on impact. Other bodies landed around her and she realised that the whole roof was falling in. She looked upward and saw darkness. The large lump of stone hit the top of her head. It immediately broke her neck, but had hit her at such an angle that it pushed the prostitute's head and neck straight down into her body. For a moment, her eyes were level with her shoulders and her mouth was gaping from where her chest should have been. Then her body slumped to the ground.

As the roof fell, it began to pull the walls of the temple inward. Masonry fell onto the terraces, landing on the crowds there.

A small boy turned to his father as he heard a grunt of pain amid the bedlam. His father was looking at him with a glazed expression. And then blood began to trickle from his nose and mouth. His father fell forward and the boy shrieked in horror. The back of his father's head was missing. The boy got up screaming and began to run with everyone else. But he was felled as a body from the roof landed on his back, pinning him to the ground and breaking his back in the process. Neither body nor boy ever moved again.

The enclosure above the main door came crashing down killing several of the Seranims instantly. All their riches and power came to nothing when walls and stone began to fall. The others, including Abad and Shennahgon, fell forward, losing their footing.

'Let me die with the Philistines!' Shimshon's cry was the last coherent thing heard, as the temple crumbled. Once again he raised his eyes to where the Seranim's should be. There is only one who cannot be looked upon and that is the God of Abraham, the God of Moses and the God of Shimshon. He thanked his God for not leaving him and for saving his people. Then he looked forward once more and smiled.

* * *

The sky had fallen on the Philistines and, thanks to the attraction of seeing Shimshon, over 3,000 were crushed that day. Shimshon himself was buried beneath the rubble, but he had killed more Philistines as he died than when he was alive.

News of the defeat of Philistia spread throughout the whole region. Shimshon's brothers brought back his body and buried him next to his father, Manoah.

Perhaps now, freed from Philistine control, Shimshon's people, God's people, would be able to follow God and give their Lord the honour and love that was due.

Or perhaps not, but that is another story.

Note for the reader

The events depicted in *The Sky Will Fall* are based on the stories recorded in Judges 13–16. The author has woven these stories together with historical and archeological evidence of life in Israel around the 12th century BC to help you explore the difficult questions that the Bible text raises.

Read the Bible passages about Samson, his loves and his battles and reflect on what they tell you about God. What is God saying to you through these stories? If you have any questions, find a Christian you trust and chat through your ideas, thoughts and concerns.

What are Dark Chapters?

What is the Christian response to the vast array of horror books aimed at young people? Is it to condemn these titles and ban them from our shelves? Is it to ignore this trend and let our young people get on with reading them? At Scripture Union, we believe this presents a fantastic opportunity to help young people get into the pages of God's Word and wrestle with some of the difficult questions of faith.

The text does not sensationalise the horrific aspects of each story for entertainment's sake, and therefore trivialise what the story has to say. On the contrary, each retold account uses the more fantastic and gruesome epsiodes of each character's story to grip the reader and draw them into assessing why these events take place.

The reader is asked throughout the books to consider questions about the nature of God, how we should live as Christians, what value we place on things of this world – power, wealth, influence or popularity – and what God values.

For additional information and resources, visit
www.scriptureunion.org.uk/darkchapters

The Egyptian Nightmare

'Thus says the Lord, the God of Israel, "Let my people go that they may celebrate a feast to me in the wilderness."'

There's a moment of silence that feels much longer than it really is. It's one of those moments where everyone wishes they were somewhere, anywhere else. Pharaoh is the only one unfazed. He takes his time before responding icily.

'Who is "the Lord" that I should obey his voice to let Israel go?' Then he raises his voice so that it resounds powerfully through the courtyard. 'I do not know the Lord!'

Pharaoh is ruler of all he surveys. His kingdom is prosperous and his monuments are being built at a fantastic rate by his Hebrew slaves. But suddenly, Moses and Aaron appear in his palace and demand the release of God's people. As events spiral out of his control and God strikes his country with terrifying plagues, Pharaoh's desperate attempts to regain power only lead to his own destruction.

978 1 84427 535 9
£5.99

Izevel, Queen of Darkness

Izevel fell, fell and fell. She looked frantically downwards.

Around her, with outstretched arms of flame, and pale, decaying, ghastly faces, were the beings she had loved to worship. And they were laughing; hideous, screaming laughter. In one despairing moment she realised, too late, that they had lied to her all her life and she had believed them. Her Nightmares had come to claim her for ever.

Slowly, slowly, slowly, Izevel, Princess of Tyre, works her influence over her new husband, Ahav, and his kingdom Israel. Leading them away from Adonai, she encourages the unspeakable practices of Baal worship. But despite her best efforts, the Lord and his prophets will not be disposed of so easily. Increasingly driven mad by her own lifestyle, Izevel races headlong towards her own grisly downfall.

978 1 84427 536 6
£5.99